A NOVEL

A HUNDRED

SILENT

WAYS

MARI JOJIE

RIVER GROVE
BOOKS

This book is a work of fiction. Names, characters, businesses, organizations, places, events, and incidents are either a product of the author's imagination or are used fictitiously. Any resemblance to actual persons, living or dead, events, or locales is entirely coincidental.

Published by River Grove Books
Austin, TX
www.rivergrovebooks.com

Distributed by River Grove Books

Design and composition by Greenleaf Book Group
Cover design by Greenleaf Book Group
Cover images used under license from
©Shutterstock.com/Vikoshkina; ©Shutterstock.com/
Ovchinnkov Vladimir

Publisher's Cataloging-in-Publication data is available.

Print ISBN: 978-1-63299-370-0

eBook ISBN: 978-1-63299-371-7

First Edition

A HUNDRED

SILENT

WAYS

For Isabel and Jacob, the two best parts of me.
My life and joy. I'm reassured with the thought
that a tree is known by its fruit.

For Patrick, the love that is gentle, constant, and true.
I love you then. Now. And for all the days to come.

For my mom and my dad,
the core that kept me from getting broken.

I write about love because I've been surrounded by it.

CHAPTER 1

When You Wait Out a Storm

"I like a look of agony, because I know it's true."

—Emily Dickinson

Summer 2016

was wearing my reliable black ballet flats. Tatty but comfy, they were an easy pick as I hurriedly left the house. They went well with my slinky black leggings that I wore all the time. I owned three of them, so it was a no-brainer as I grabbed a pair to put on for this trip and threw on a white cotton shirt and red cardigan. In fact, it took little mental effort to decide what to wear. Just as it did when I tinkered over the details of how exactly I would run away.

It was an early morning in August. I didn't anticipate the frigid air, although I had a hunch that it was not the temperature that was making me shiver. I was anxious, but I also felt I had reached a point of no return. The plane ticket I'd paid for was nonrefundable. And my marriage was over. I supposed there could be more to be gained by moving forward than retracing my steps back to where things fell apart.

I stood at a corner near my house, waiting for my cab. It was eerily dark and quiet. But the dread in my heart was far greater than the fear of getting mugged. The headlights of an approaching car suddenly dimmed as the vehicle got closer. When it halted in front of me, I climbed in without hesitation.

"To LAX, please."

· · ·

At the Tokyo Narita International Airport, the looping announcements of canceled flights resulted in loud grunts and heavy sighs among the people around me. Everyone was on a roundabout with the outbound flights temporarily grounded due to the approaching Typhoon Lionrock. But this was no merry-go-round. It was a carousel of frustrated travelers.

I had just gotten off the plane, and had anticipated only a short break in my journey when I heard my connecting flight to the Philippines had been delayed. There was no way to escape this storm, as the typhoon had just left my final destination. I would have to wait it out. Besides, the storm that was hovering over Tokyo gave me a perfect reason to hide. Who would have thought that a crowded space could provide me a quiet refuge? It was probably the effect of knowing I was at a standstill.

My spirit was sapped and adrift as I hustled along in the direction where everyone seemed to be headed. I was recounting the bitter turn of events with my head bowed as my eyes watched my steps stay on with the crowd. When I reached a busy pocket of noodle shops and food bars and saw the dummy food displays, my stomach started to gurgle—I had not eaten for almost a day. My head throbbed from hunger and my eyes were burning.

Reaching a dead end, I instinctively went to my right side, the dominant side that insisted upon a creative but less organized way of thinking. Without giving it much thought, I ordered the first thing I saw—menu #1, shoyu ramen. Even if it was written in the English alphabet, I struggled with making this decision, because I saw no purpose to anything. Should I start leaving everything to chance, or to the first option to come up?

The dine-in café was not packed, but the small space meant I would have to share a table with a stranger. My hands were already trembling, perhaps due to lack of food or just sheer exhaustion, so I scanned the room quickly to find a table I could rest the heavy food tray on. And a seat to rest my tired body.

My burning eyes sought solace in the even pattern of a plaid shirt to my left. The guy wearing the shirt seemed oblivious to the world around him, his eyes set on a book. To the right was a guy in a dark gray business suit. He looked pleasant enough, until he caught me headed toward his table and decidedly looked away, as if unwilling to share his space. I made a second pivot to my left and found the plaid-shirt guy staring at me. My logical side told me his plate was almost empty—he might be done with the table soon. He also motioned his hand to the empty chair next to him, a seeming invitation.

I walked toward the guy in the plaid shirt. "Thank you," I said politely as I joined him. He gave me a weak smile. I coyly brushed off the uneasy stares between us and scooped the porcelain spoon of broth into my parched mouth. My body needed this tinge of warmth and this resting spot. And perhaps even a humdrum conversation.

"Is your flight also delayed?" I asked.

The man tentatively nodded, then gave away an earnest smile. His golden-caramel hair, which was short but textured and spiky on top, and cleanly trimmed on the sides, complemented his light honey-brown eyes. His eyes, cinched with laugh lines, spoke of forbearance—I assessed him to be the good-natured type who gave out a polite smile instead of disparaging words. The short stubble concealed some wrinkled scars. And the deeply bronzed skin must have been from days spent lounging in the sun. I didn't realize that I was staring at him until he began to move. He stood up to reveal a good-looking physique, tall and impressively fit. He then left the table without saying a word, leaving his army-like backpack slung across the back of his chair.

I was somewhat ill at ease at how disheveled I must have appeared after the lengthy flight between Los Angeles and Tokyo. My long hair was visibly tangled at the ends and tousled in a mess representative of my state of mind, and my usually amber skin was pale and dry. When I peered into the reflective glass next to me, my black eyes revealed nothing but my overcast emotion. Not that I needed to be pretty, just not miserable looking or shabby.

Plaid-shirt guy came back with two chilled bottles of Asahi. He offered me one, placing it next to my water, so I gave away another "thank you." I thought it would be wise to manage my headache before drinking, so I swallowed three tablets of Advil with my water, then raised my complimentary drink to propose a toast. With an outstretched arm, he briskly clinked his bottle against mine. The abruptness of his movements again caught me by surprise. He seemed calculating but had yet to speak a word to me. His gaze was intense, like a hawk's, and his responses were curt, but he somehow made me feel welcome.

There was an array of things in California—major decisions and impositions—I needed to regain control over, but I had fled—cowardly—away from it all. Twelve hours prior when I had agreed to a divorce, I was in a different city, a different country. Backtrack two days more, and I was in a different storm. Not the pouring rain kind of storm, but a downpour of miserable emotions. Part of me wanted to chat up this guy, but, in all honesty, I was not in any mood for small talk. There were too many conversations playing in my head. *Are you happy? How much longer should we stay like this? This is not working out. I am tired of waiting for you. Tired of being the only one who wants this.* I had no energy left in me.

I looked around the café in hopes of distracting myself from my inner wallowing, taking in the various people seated around me. I proceeded to finish my breakfast, even if it was already past seven—nighttime in Tokyo. Without appearing ungrateful or rude, I hurriedly gulped down the crisp but dry Japanese lager. It seemed natural to assume that this guy had put a stake at this table and was in no rush to leave, so it was probably appropriate that I excuse myself and give him his space.

"Thank you again for sharing the table and the beer," I told him. As I collected my oversized tote bag, he hurriedly placed his phone in front of me. In a medium-sized font, it read, *I am Deaf. I don't mean to sound uninterested.* It was ironic how he used "Deaf" and "sound" in the same breath. I put my bag back on the chair and wondered what to say. Words that he wouldn't be able to hear. Words I wouldn't be able to explain without sound.

Offering him my best candid smile—in order to avoid appearing astounded—I typed my name, Kate, on his app and returned the phone to him. He quickly flashed his name to me—William. I managed to stop myself from blurting out that he shared the same name as my son. I was not ready to reveal this personal detail yet. He then added, "Call me Liam."

After some exchanges of messages, Liam texted, "I can read lips, not minds." I found this heartwarming enough to elicit a giggle. It was not my plan to stay on for another round of drinks, but I did—this time he got me a handcrafted matcha green tea. I decided to hang out with Liam. It was interesting spending time with him. Though I could not hear his voice, I felt his every word. He made me stop thinking of the brewing typhoon, the ten hours I had to wait for the flight, the mess I had left behind in California. By chance, he was also waiting for the same flight to Manila. I thought nothing of this coincidence except as a lucky break—I didn't think being alone in my misery was a healthy option for me, and here he was, someone to be with.

"Tell me what your speaking voice is like." I received this message from Liam.

"I spoke Filipino before I learned English, so I probably have an accent but not as thick as my mom's." Sent. Then I added, "I am not high-pitched. Nor baritone. I guess whatever is in the middle."

"Didn't think you were high-pitched. I sensed a calm talker in you."

I looked up and found him watching me, so I turned my attention back to my phone. "Were you born Deaf?" But I hesitated, then deleted this. "How long has it been?" Deleted again. "Can you hear anything at all?" Sent.

"I can hear my thoughts. LOL"

It was easier to react to exaggerated claims than deprecating honesty. I didn't know what to say to this so I asked, "How long has it been?"

"I wasn't born Deaf. So, I have heard what raindrops and thunder sound like. And gunshots. I also know the sound of my name—Liam Walker—but I have never met a Kate. I don't think I have pronounced your name before. But I still know the sound of K and T."

It was not that his gaze was rude or carried any judgment. Whenever I looked up to find him still watching me, a blush of heat swarmed my face and neck. I felt unsure of myself, but I probably came across as disturbed by his gaze more than self-conscious, because he sent this message voluntarily. "I stare at you because I try to lip-read. I don't want to miss a word in case."

I was even more flustered that Liam sensed my discomfort. My flushed face must have turned pale because Liam proceeded to apologize. "Sorry."

"Don't be."

"What music do you listen to?"

I thought long and hard on his question. Should I give him a specific song? I was never good at defining myself to other people. Half of the time, I couldn't make out what things set me apart from others. "I like sad, slow songs. Nothing specific comes to mind." Then I bounced it back to him, "Do you remember the last song you heard?"

"Not the last song. But it's been stuck in my head. I feel funny even telling you this." He then added, "One of the few songs stuck in my head for at least five years now."

There was a lull from his text, so I hurled this at him, "You're killing me. What is it?"

"'Sexual Eruption' by Snoop Dogg. Wish I was joking."

The embarrassed look on his face said everything.

I couldn't believe that two hours had passed. I yawned. I pulled my legs out from under me and stretched my arms, then blurted out, "Let's walk around," to which he replied with both hands flat, facing his chest, as he moved them alternately in upward-downward circular motion. He proceeded to smile, stood up, and grabbed his backpack. I took that to be a yes. I wondered if he really was this good at reading lips.

The mad rush had died down, the space suddenly seeming devoid of energy. Most of the travelers at the terminal had been stuck for hours, and everyone seemed resigned and stoic, locked within their own zone. Compared to earlier, everyone seemed to share a similar mood now—gloomy like the city skyline of Tokyo.

We walked side by side, with enough distance between us to avoid letting our arms brush against each other. I realized I could hear footsteps from people trailing behind us as they got closer. It dawned on me that I could only rely on such an awareness because of my hearing, and not my sight, sense of touch, or smell. Liam didn't have that capacity to alert him, or to allow him to be mindful of people coming up behind him. It had to be tough—all of it—even though he tried to downplay the enormity of the hurdles when I inquired about them earlier.

"Is it hard to lip-read?"

"Depending on how big the mouth is."

"How do you manage to travel by yourself?"

"Why would it be hard? I have legs." He then added a smiley face.

"Do you live alone?"

"I've never been happy to tell anyone that I live alone until now."

When we passed by a gift shop, I hurriedly pulled his hand in that direction. I wanted to get a book or a magazine—something obvious or perceptible that would function as an excuse to detach myself from Liam. But the gesture of grabbing his hand seemed contradictory to my intent. I went straight to the corner where the reading materials were while he motioned his hand as if to say he would just roam around the store.

Oddly, the first book I picked up was about a blind French girl, so I placed it back on the rack. Without giving it much thought, I decided to grab *After You*, the sequel to Jojo Moyes' emotional story. I supposed it would be nice to get distracted by someone's heartache besides mine.

Liam was already waiting for me in a corner as I lined up to pay for the book.

My attention wandered again. It was as if I wanted time to pass more quickly, or even just for the queue to hurry up, but another part of me was helplessly trapped in the moment. I meant to tell Liam that he didn't need to wait, but I decided against it. It sounded dismissive. As if he was really a keen mind reader, I received a message.

"Take your time. I'll wait for you. I've nowhere else to go." I chuckled to myself over how he lied about not being able to read minds.

. . .

We got separated when we were boarding the plane. I purposely avoided Liam during the entire flight. I saw him again as I slogged my tired body on my way out of the airport in Manila. He was standing next to the baggage carousel, waiting patiently with hands on his pockets and his chin lowered to his chest. I didn't have any checked luggage, so I proceeded to the exit. I looked away before he had a chance to see me. I took my phone out and sent this to him, "It's nice to meet you, Liam. I'm married so this will be my last message."

CHAPTER 2

When There Was You and Me

"And would it have been worth it, after all. After
the cups, the marmalade, the tea. Among the
porcelain, among some talk of you and me."
—T. S. Eliot

California, Summer 2007

I avoided the bright, big screen, as it would only delay tweaking my vision and allowing it to adapt to the darkened space. The movie previews were already finished when I walked in. I had always found it rude when people came in late, marching in front of the screen and blocking everyone's view of it, and that was why it didn't feel right to even be choosy about where to sit. I went to the first open chair I spotted.

One of my favorite things to do alone was go to the cinema, and I was serious about it. I hated it when movie dialogues were drowned out by distracting noises. If I wanted to socialize, I would instead go to a bar with friends. Because I had skipped lunch earlier, I was eagerly munching on my buttered popcorn. I was immersed with Allison and Ben's unexpected hookup when I mistakenly took the wrong drink. I almost spit it at the guy next to me, the owner of the drink, before profusely apologizing to him. He laughed as he said, "Don't worry about it" in an exaggeratedly soft voice as a hint that I was making unnecessary noise with the nonstop sorry.

This awkward mistake actually broke the ice for us. After grabbing his drink, it felt more like I was watching this movie with a cozy date. We glanced at each other while laughing, or made soft side comments as if we were well acquainted. When the lights came back on, we flashed each other a nice-to-finally-meet-you smile. We walked to the exit door almost side by side as the conversation progressed effortlessly.

He initiated the introduction. "By the way," he said. "I'm Kyle."

"Kate. Nice to meet you." I did a nice-to-meet-you wave. I had always found handshakes to be too formal and manly.

"Since you were too embarrassed to take my drink, how about I get you a new one?"

"Oh. I can't tonight." It came out curtly, which was not my intention at all.

"Ah." He paused. "Well, Kate, hope to see you again sometime."

"Oh, it's not a brush off," I immediately said. To sound more encouraging, I continued, "I just can't tonight. I need to drop off food to a friend's house."

"Is that friend a boyfriend?" His inquisitive look provoked an I-got-caught reflex on my part, as if I was being dishonest. I was never a cheat. I would never be like my past boyfriends.

"An ex-boyfriend. But the food is not for him—it's for his mom. He pays me to drop off dinner for her whenever he works nights."

"Interesting. Well, I'm meeting friends at Conchita's. It's a going-away dinner. Otherwise I would ditch it for you. Do you want to join us if it's a quick errand?"

"But we just met," I reasoned coyly.

"So, what's wrong with that? How long before you'll agree to a dinner?"

"Next time. Not tonight. Enjoy your time with your friends." I sounded genuine. After he walked me to my car and we had exchanged mobile numbers, and he had driven off, I was instantly disappointed by my decision.

• • •

It was as easy and refreshing as the breeze, getting to know Kyle. We continued our dispatch of probing messages throughout the night after we separated, and through the succeeding days. He was never short of questions for me. Those revealed more about him than what my answers could ever give away about me. Truth be told, there was nothing extraordinary about me. Somehow, people mistook my vagueness as being enigmatic. Even more bewilderingly, people found it appealing.

"Why are you not with someone?"—one of Kyle's text messages.

"Back at you. Why aren't you too?"

"I meant, you're attractive. Hot. You seem caring. To say you're a catch is not an exaggeration."

"So, you're basically asking, what's wrong with me?"

"LOL Well . . . if you put it that way . . . Sorry for my tendency to get to the bottom of things. I didn't mean to be intrusive."

I postponed replying at first, then decided to totally ignore his comment. Partly because the lunch crowd at the bakeshop I worked at had already overwhelmed me.

When this tall, long-legged, and equally long-necked brunette walked in—as she did almost religiously every Sunday—I dropped my phone in my apron pocket. She was the type who brought along the sun with her, shimmering as she walked into a space. She was not rude, or snotty, but she was the impatient type. And a classic indecisive shopper. The type who pointed to the display glass shelf as she looked out to the parking lot, perhaps to her forbearing boyfriend, to ask for an opinion. She proceeded to call whoever she deemed critical to the decision-making process, and spent the next five minutes polling for a consensus.

"Do we want a muffin or cupcake? Do we want an apple crumble or banana caramel? But do we want carrot muffins too?"

I patiently listened to her plummy voice while making a mental guess on how this mini-survey would still wind up in indecision.

In the end, she would get one of each. I wondered how she stayed fit. Perhaps she only ate on Sundays. And as soon as she paid, she then remembered. "Oh, panini! That's what my boyfriend wanted." Meanwhile, she had already created a line of peeved customers, teeming up to the entrance door.

"Are you still ignoring me?" I received the message three days after our last text exchange. Vaguely, it seemed we were playing what a staring contest was for texting. As if whoever blinked first said a lot about a person. But in this instance, with Kyle reaching out first even when I brushed off his message, it projected something about him—that he was perhaps patient and not proud, or that he could be genuinely interested in me. So, I followed this with a reply and shared a little bit about myself. It was a reward for yielding. "I was the supportive girlfriend of a med student. So supportive that I forgot about myself, so now it's the all-about-me phase."

"Then you should stop being the errand girl."

I wondered if I should give him the benefit of the doubt for genuinely looking out for me, or pigeonhole him as being overbearing or suspicious. "Are you jealous?"

"Not yet. But I can be." The admission of potential jealousy seemed rather intense—we had just met, after all.

Exactly a week after, Kyle suggested dinner at La Dolce Vita, and I found myself putting forth a major-league effort. I curled the edges of my hair, then gently ran my fingers through for a messy, no-effort guise. Paired with my most tight-fitting jeans was a stretchy peachy-nude-colored shirt that boosted my bosom. Its creamy tone blended well with my skin, I thought. Dusted on my cheeks was a light coral powder blush, to match my champagne-pink lip gloss. Sprayed on my pulse points was Jo Malone nectarine blossoms and honey cologne, which I frugally used only on occasions when I wanted to feel sexy. I supposed I was old enough, at twenty-four, for a racy night. I said this to myself as I fixed my bra to push my boobs up while drowning out the incessant unsolicited advice of my conservative mom in my head, "Kate, save yourself for marriage."

The restaurant was a vintage historical house converted into a relaxed dating spot—on those evenings when it was not hosting a wedding or wine tasting. It was a little crowded because of an out-door concert scheduled at the Downtown Heritage Square flanking the restaurant. The evening breeze shimmied my hair, hints of sweet floral fragrance exuding from my washed tresses. Couples deep in conversation crammed the open space, and soft yellow string lights added to a romantic ambience. Waiting by the entrance, Kyle was a delight to watch. I felt a tinge of excitement as I walked toward him. He was only a few inches taller than me, which made him seem accessible, like we were in the same league. He was clean-shaven—bare and marvelously smooth. The ash brown crew cut was a great match to his inverted-triangle face that led to a sharp point at his chin—his sexiest feature.

Like me, Kyle had made an effort to look good. As we traded excited greetings, he went in for a kiss on my cheek, then whispered in an enthralled voice, "You smell sinfully sweet." If that line was any indication, Kyle was working his way to get into my pants. Typically, this would have offended me, but the glow in his steely hazel eyes took me to where those lines were supposed to make me feel—whisked away.

The dinner was elegant. The conversation was playful. It started when Kyle declared to the server, "I'll get whatever she's having." He winked, and I couldn't help but wonder if the gesture was for me or for the bubbly waitress.

"And why is that?" I asked, when it was just the two of us again at the table.

"I want to see how great you are at making choices."

Was he being cocky or playful? It was hard to tell. "Ahh. I didn't think I was being surveyed."

"Oh, believe me. We're way too overdressed if this is supposed to qualify as surveying."

"Huh." It was all that I managed to say as I lifted my mouth in a smirk.

The mood the entire evening was flirtatious. After dinner, the outdoor concert bought us time to figure out what to do next. The live music added to the stirring dynamics of our night while the crowd pushed us to stand intimately closer. When I whispered something to Kyle, he turned his face toward me right to a point where his lips were directly aligned with mine. Within seconds, his enthused mouth tenderly sucked my lips. His encouraging hands swooped me in a snug embrace. Within the hour, we were back at his nearby apartment, unthinkingly undressed—his mouth all over my elated body while his fingers gently rubbed my craved, soaked spot. As he was about to launch himself on top of me, Kyle managed to ask, "Is it okay?" in an utmost gentlemanly hiss that elicited a fit of giggles from me. He was a poster boy of politeness.

Once I managed to quiet down, he was breathing hard in frustration, while I had teared up from excessive laughter. I realized then that I had never been treated this tenderly, which left me unable to recognize his sincerity. I'd never met someone decent like Kyle. We found ourselves lying side by side, our eyes fixed to the popcorn ceiling of his bedroom.

"I'm sorry. It must have been annoying to hear me laugh as if you said something funny." I tried my best to sound sincere.

Kyle did not attempt to hide his irritation at all. "It's alright," he said moodily. "I just didn't know what to make of it. Do you want me to walk you back to your car now?"

In an attempt to woo him back, I turned up on my knees with my legs on the sides of his hip bones. I was widely spread out to reveal the eagerness that was being ignored. As I touched the same spot he was gently rubbing earlier, I decided that it was my turn to ask, "May I?" Kyle pushed himself up to my wet opening as I welcomed him in and rode passionately. He watched me enjoy myself before laying me on my back, my legs flung to his shoulders. It was now his turn to set the pace, and he plunged into my abyss.

To relinquish all the uncertainties was not so frightening after all. It shouldn't have mattered that I had surrendered all my pawns in chess—contrary to what my mom said—as long as the queen was still next to the king.

"I'm sorry about earlier. I overreact whenever I feel attacked or laughed at."

"I wasn't making fun of you."

"I realize that, but I've already ruined the mood."

"Aren't you the sensitive one?" I said.

"Partly due to growing up in a large household with many bossy older brothers. Nothing miserable or abusive."

"What was that like?"

"We got paid for doing household chores. But then we also had to pay for every meal we consumed. Even breakfast cereal."

"Wow," I said. "That's tough."

It was Kyle's turn to laugh at me as he clarified, "I was just messing with you."

"Not cool, Kyle."

"Okay . . . sorry. This one's an actual recollection of my childhood. I was never invited back for fishing with my dad and older brothers because I almost drowned the first time that they took me. It was a near-death experience."

"Aw. Poor boy."

"Yup, that's why I hate fishing. And sushi." Kyle went on to ask, "Tell me a childhood memory."

"Let me think . . . Oh, I remember when I was younger, I walked in on my parents having sex."

"Whoa . . . that's messed up!"

With a puppy face, I proceeded to say, "Huh! Not true." I laughed as I said, "I was just messing with you too!"

"Ah, good one. Know what I find sexiest—you just know when to return the compliment and when to strike back," he said, moving his hand under the blanket that covered me and stroking my thighs with his fingers. Once his digits were on my flora, and I started to moan again, he abruptly stopped and whispered, "Now, tell me something more and I'll guess if it's true or bluff before we go on."

That threw me off for a second. Ultra-sensitive one minute, then douchey the next! But I could play this game too.

I took his right palm and pretended that I could read his fortune.

"These two lines here that are intertwined mean that you're mind over heart."

"I don't know about that." Kyle challenged my reading.

I took his left hand to compare. "This line here," I said, pointing at a faint line on the side of his palm just below his index finger, "this one tells me that you'll be married before the age of thirty. In fact, might be happening soon."

Kyle clarified any miscalculations I may have about his age. "But, I'm just twenty-four."

Then I progressed to stroke his middle and index fingers as I mischievously claimed, "This is the finger of Saturn. This is the finger of Jupiter. I can tell in confidence where they both belong. Right here in my Venus."

Kyle was amused and equally pleased to oblige.

By and large, we hit it off straightaway. We stopped going to the cinemas alone and became movie buddies. We became lovers and best of friends. Kyle and I were inseparable and crazy about each other from there on out. As spontaneously as our initial meeting at the movie theater, I got knocked-up the following summer. And hitched soon after.

CHAPTER 3

When You Do Not Plan Your Trip Well

"Filipinos don't realize that victory is the child of struggle, that joy blossoms from suffering, and redemption is a product of sacrifice."

—Jose Rizal

A couple of nights prior to booking my escape flight, I had a vivid dream of myself—I couldn't categorically mark this as just a dream because it was laid out almost just the way it happened. I was twelve, hiding in my room. Head buried in a pillow, forbidding tears from brimming and anger from bursting. There was nothing a daughter could do to stop her disparaged father from conceding to defeat. Their decision to separate made sense. They were both unhappy. They were both miserable with their roles reversed—she was the breadwinner and he the home-maker. Perhaps it was a cultural thing. Or simply ego on his side. But it was hurting them both.

My father stowed his life away in two suitcases. My mother, tired from her night duty as a nurse, buried her sadness in much-needed sleep. When the airport shuttle arrived to pick him up, my dad knocked at my bedroom door, desperately. Begged for me to hug him goodbye. Left with no choice, I went downstairs to join him for one last moment. I refused to meet his miserable eyes but oblig-ingly listened to his measured parting statements, with my head bent downward and my long hair all sprawled forward to conceal my sorrow.

"Kate, take care of yourself. Remember that I love you. I just can't bear how my life turned out here, so it's best to go home. I'll leave you with Mom . . . not because I don't love you. On the contrary, I do. And that's why I'll leave you with her. She's able to give you a better life here."

As soon as I bolted the door, I ran to the powder room to splash water on my tear-stained face. The bathroom in my dream looked just as I remembered it did, except when I raised my head from the sink, it was my son, Willy, on the other side of the mirror. Gasping for breath, I coiled up from my sleep. I had been dreaming.

That dream jolted me out of the bed. I tried to forget about the fate of my marriage by muffling myself to sleep, just to be woken up this way. Seated on the bed with my back on the headboard, I returned to the inevitable question—what now? Within the hour, I made a few impulsive choices. I had not done anything like this in a long time. In the dead of the night, I booked a flight to

Manila, Philippines. Left the house without a word and without packing any luggage.

When I arrived at the Los Angeles Airport, I sent an apologetic message to Doris at work for dropping the ball. I called my dad, asking if I could stay with him for a few days. Then, I sent two text messages before I turned off my mobile. The first one was for Mom, and read, *Please do not be too worried and will call when ready to talk.* The second was for Kyle. It read, *You're right, let's get a divorce.*

• • •

My biological father almost failed to recognize me, his only child, at least as far as I know of. We had lost touch ever since he decided to walk out of my life, and Mom's.

A year after he left California, he sent me a letter. It contained basically the same things he said that day when he left. He didn't make many promises—not even that he would stay in touch. In fact, it was the complete opposite. He promised that he would stay away from our lives if it would make things easier. What that meant, then and now, was lost on me. He stayed away for two years, until my fifteenth birthday when I received a card. The fading colors of the ink and the abating form of the envelope suggested that it had traveled far. His words sounded more repentant. But by then, my father had started to be like a mere photograph— evidence of a past event. At that age, I was self-sufficient. He kept sending birthday cards every year from that point on, at least for a few more years until they stopped coming. Curiously, the last birthday card bore a phone number and he said that if and when I decided to call, he would be on the other end, notwithstanding half the world away, receiving it. Had he finally given up on me, after a handful of attempts, and did this imply that the ball was now in my court?

Like a child abandoned by a parent, perhaps similar to one that has been given up for adoption, I had my doubts when I tried calling that number as soon as I left the house, and continued to do so a few more times, up until I arrived at LAX. I braced myself for another disappointment, doubting whether he even cared about me, or that he'd kept the same number all these years. What were the odds of either?

"I knew he was a flake," I said, shaking my head in frustration the first time I punched in the number on my mobile.

From the moment I purchased the ticket, arranged for a cab to take me to the airport, and checked myself in for the flight, everything felt like it was working in my favor until I realized I had no place to go to once in Manila if I was unable to reach my dad. I flicked through the throngs of passengers deciding on whom to ask for help. I had to befriend a *tita*, an aunt, a term Filipinos easily accord any female stranger as a sign of respect and commonality. I chose to approach this lady who looked to be quite nosy, watching everyone who passed by her side. She might welcome a small chat to relieve herself of curiosity, if not boredom. As it turned out, I was using the wrong country code.

"Oh, it's a landline. Okay, you do this." *Great, a busy tone.*

She crossed out the numbers she wrote down on her small notepad and wrote a new set. "Oh, it's in Metro Manila. Okay, you do this."

I finally heard an old-fashioned, classic ring tone. With an excited smile, I told her, "Hey, Tita. I think I'm connecting." Connecting to the other line. Half the world away. To my surprised father. Twenty years later.

• • •

As soon as I heard a gruff voice, I overexcitedly screeched out a "hello." Without wasting another second, I inquired for my father. "I'm looking for Juancho Pineda."

"Who's calling?"

"Kate." I hesitated, then went on to elaborate. "Kate Pineda."

The rough, low tone quickly turned into a tremble as the voice on the other line finally replied to ask, "Is that really you, Kate? Is that really you, my child?" It was hard to mistake the sound of disbelief in his voice for anything other than a nice, surprised feeling.

"Yes, it's me." I breathed in as I took in this mammoth mix of a dream and palpable occurrence. My mind was clouded on what else to say to fill in the gap in our voices so I just got to the point. "Will it be okay to visit and stay with you?"

The reunion over the phone was heartfelt. It hit me like the warmth of the sun during wintertime. My father sounded as I remembered. Then and there, I felt that sharp pinch again in my heart, the way it felt whenever I saw a father dropping off his child at the school bus, or a father seated on a bench watching his child toss a ball.

As soon as I ended the call, Tita peppered me with her curiosity. She must have picked up the thrill in my voice and the balminess in my expression. The same sentiments were now speckled in the way she eyed me intently. "What did your father say? Is he picking you up? He should." But then she fleetingly switched gears, turning the positivity on its head. "It's hard to get a taxi at the airport. And with your accent, the taxi driver might charge you more."

"For my accent?"

"Well, you will sound like you only carry dollar bills, so they might charge you, say fifty dollars. It's either fifty dollars or two thousand pesos. If I ask you right now, in an instant, which will you pick?"

"Fifty dollars?" I said tentatively.

"See, you're not ready to take a taxi. We can't blame the driver—he didn't trick you. You didn't negotiate. And you don't know the value of dollars in pesos. Oh my! You're not ready to be left alone in Manila."

Tita scared me a bit. Thankfully, my dad took my call and agreed to pick me up. Thankfully, I have a dad in Manila. Somehow, this little unexpected gratitude washed away all the resentments bottled inside my heart. I had forgiven my biological dad within an instant. I was just a product of sacrifice, after all.

Tita never left my side, as if we were traveling together, except when she had to use the restroom—then she would ask me to stay with her carry-on suitcase. "Please look after my bag *ha*?" I nodded without reluctance. It was the least I could do in return for her help with the call to my father. She was nice and all, but I needed to be left alone, so I purposely avoided Tita once we reached Tokyo, hurrying away without looking back the minute I stepped off the ramp and into the airport.

When she saw me with Liam at the outbound gate in Narita, she had that questioning look on her face. Almost a judgment. As a ruse to avoid her glances, I decided to close my eyes and pretended to sleep. Until the pretend turned into forty winks. If I was snoring, I wouldn't have known. If the plane to Manila left without me, I wouldn't have known. Liam was next to me, so I was not worried. It was a comforting thought.

The conversation with Tita played back in my head as I struggled to shut my mind off these looping worries. The realities I had to confront, and how I didn't plan this trip well. Who would have thought that a cab would cost me that much? I'd be done after twenty cab rides, and probably wouldn't last longer than ten days! My return flight was in three weeks. Would I be ready to fly back then? And would I even survive three weeks of being away from home? In any case, I needed some more spending money to survive without tapping on our joint savings. I'd have to rely on my credit card, which was probably close to maxing out.

I hadn't planned this trip very well at all.

The onslaught of financial worries fell so heavily upon me that I drifted into a deep sleep. Liam gently shook me to mean that it was time. The loud intercom speakers said what Liam could not express, "Boarding in ten minutes."

We stood next to each other in line. Like Liam, I refused to open my mouth to talk, though my reason was hygienic. If there was even a slight chance of his being interested in me, it would be gone as soon as he got a whiff of my morning breath.

• • •

When we landed in Manila, I made several decisions—first, to stop thinking about Kyle and our divorce; second, to stop messaging Liam; and third, to stop hating my father. When it took my biological dad a long second to realize that I was his daughter, I was saddened but not surprised.

"I must look so different from when I was twelve. You didn't recognize me right away." My father was embarrassed to admit this so
I tried my best to sound cool about it. If it was Mom, she would still
have recognized me. In an instant. Then again, this scenario would
never happen because she would never have abandoned me in the
first place. Oh, I can't hate my father for this.

My father and I hugged awkwardly, like estranged families at
a belated reunion. Or two complete strangers who had just survived a grave accident, still disoriented to do much but hug. He still
looked exactly the same as the man picked up by that airport shuttle
two decades ago, except that his hair was now salt and pepper. And
there were more worry lines on his forehead and right around his
soft-spoken eyes.

"*Napagod ka ba sa byahe?*" He was asking me if I was tired from
the flight.

"Yes."

"*May pamilya ka na ba?*"

"Yes, I have a family. Mom remarried." The look on his face as
he quickly glanced at me revealed that this was news to him. I realized that I needed to choose my words more carefully—my state of
exhaustion was making this difficult.

It was a few moments of uneasy silence when he continued
with the conversation, probing. "Not your mom. You, you. Are you
married?"

"Yes." I was starting to dislike this getting-to-know-you chat.

"*Anak?* Do you have kids?"

I chewed on this the way he did when I accidentally revealed that
Mom remarried. I felt sad that my son had never met my biological

father. And that my biological father didn't even know I had a son. "Yes," I told him, then I paused. "William."

"That's great to hear!" He couldn't contain his excitement. "Later, show me picture *ha*."

I gave out a heavy sigh. "Yeah, later, Dad."

Earlier, when I was outside at the airport, and even in the thick of the crowd, there had been a humid waft carted along by a faint breeze—it had felt tolerable compared to the stagnant air in my dad's outmoded Mitsubishi Galant, which had a very languid AC. That, or it had somehow been defectively wired to be a heater rather than a cooling system. Though I knew this to be impossible, it sure felt that way. Sweat was beginning to roll off my body. I was wiping off my face and nape when my dad asked, "*Masama ba pakiramdam mo?*"

"No, I don't resent you."

He laughed nervously. "No, no . . . sick . . . Are you sick? Because you were touching your head."

"Oh, I'm wiping my sweat off."

"Do you mind the *alikabok*?"

"Oh, is that the orange noodle with the anchovies?"

"No, that's called *palabok*. I was referring to the dust, *alikabok*. If you're okay with the dust, then I can turn off the AC, open the window."

"Yes, I think it's better to roll down the window."

The streets of Manila still bore puddles of water from the storm. Added to that were deep potholes, which made for a rough ride. The slow traffic saved the majority of the pedestrians from getting splashed by the remaining rainwater flooding those potholes. Those who walked dangerously close alongside moving vehicles still got wet, which, unfortunately, was something drivers could not avoid. The street was very packed, especially with the thick mob of foot travelers walking briskly, leaving little room to maneuver. Interestingly, the narrow street that was supposedly a one-lane each way became four lanes of piled-up vehicles patiently doing a stop-and-go.

"Good thing we had the storm, therefore not dusty. Asthma, you still have?"

The silver lining. It's what enduring people see after a calamity. Rainfall meant free water for the agriculture, except when it's a bad typhoon. But bad typhoons turned Filipinos into an enduring culture and children of struggles who were never blind to the small victories of life. Silver linings.

"Not as bad as when I was young." Asthma should be the last thing my dad needed to worry about for me.

After two hours of traveling a forty-mile distance, we finally arrived at a very slender alleyway, and my dad began to turn into it. Entering looked like an impossible mission. "We can just walk if we're near your house now, instead of forcing your car into this narrow street."

"Oh, don't worry." Dad reassured me that even garbage trucks used this thoroughfare. He honked rowdily and the red accordion gate slid open. He maneuvered the car directly alongside sidewalls, metal gates, and houses—all of which he could easily run into. But he didn't smash into any of these. I'd never been prouder of my dad.

A burly lady in a body-hugging neon green shirt and tight denim shorts came out to greet us. She hailed us with an exaggerated smile. Her medium bob was ash brown with blonde highlights, making my hair dark compared to hers. She was very pale, almost milky white, my skin tone dark compared to hers. If she told me she was from East Asia, I wouldn't doubt it because of her complexion, which I attributed to a lifetime of herbal and oolong tea drinking. Her eyes were big and round. And her body frame was not petite. She was an attractive woman, relatively young, perhaps in her early forties. But there was something I couldn't put my finger on that slightly repulsed me. Was it her hideous shirt color? Or was it the way she welcomed me, and was now about to hug me . . .

"Are you Kate?"

"Yes." I immediately wondered if she was my half-sister.

"I'm Diday. Your dad's girlfriend."

Aha! There it was. "Hi." Did my voice crack?

"Are you hungry, already?"

Was that a complaint? "I can eat," I told her. My friendly side refused to come out.

"What you want? I buy."

What were my options? "Anything you have ready or easy," I told her.

The house was a humble structure. Cement walls held a variety of themes and decor upon them—a distractingly huge television by the entrance door that took up the entire wall of the receiving area, two bulky speakers that were feebly suspended to opposite walls like ears to a face, and a Last Supper tapestry, wrapped in clear plastic that provided reflection, like a mirror, but obscured any onlooker from seeing the artwork. Next to these were framed images of various saints including the Virgin Mary, and a vulgar wall calendar—all masking the bare natural gray tone of the wall. Though I had never considered myself claustrophobic, the low ceiling felt a little confining, or oppressive. It was a clean house overall, except for the fact that they had corners of piled stuff, which was mildly suggestive of a hoarder scenario. That, or they didn't have enough storage space.

"Come on—I show you upstairs," Diday told me.

I nodded and followed her up a tight spiral steel stairway that hurled us upstairs to an even smaller box, with two bedrooms eating up the floor plan. I hoped that the second bedroom was for me, and I paused in front of it. She started with a nervous laugh, then proceeded to say, "That's your grandma in that room, so me and you share here."

Now I could see exactly how poorly I had planned this trip.

"How's she my grandma?" It was not a large family on either side. There were very few uncles and aunts on my dad's side of the family, and both his parents had passed away before we even left for California. My mom, adopted by her aunt, was an only child. Her aunt was the only relative I knew of, and she was probably dead too. I suspected this grandma to be this neon-green lady's mom.

"Your grandma! Your family!" she said again, as if it was her mission to convince me so.

I decided to put this to the side for a more pressing issue. "Where will my dad sleep?"

"Down. Donchu' worry." But I couldn't help but be worried. I looked around, then placed my stare on the floor as I recounted the layout downstairs. But where in that tiny space? Between the wooden loveseat and coffee table, which would cramp him like a fetus, or next to the bulky dining table that left no space for people to move around it? Would it be on the kitchen floor? "*Ay,* donchu' worry. He's used to it." She said this with a click of her tongue, as if to force me to snap out of my unsettled expression.

Despite the appearance of financial struggle, the food they served was lavish. The big dining table was now covered in banana leaves and a casual banquet of white rice, fried fish, fish heads in bowls of soup, grilled pork chops, grilled shrimp, sliced green mangoes, blanched spinach, wrinkled eggplants, skinny green beans, and *bagoong*, a type of shrimp paste. It looked like we were going to be eating with our hands.

"Kate, no clothes?" A mouth full of food did not keep Diday from talking.

"No."

"Why?" My father shushed her, so Diday said, "Sorry."

Diday, like the tita at the airport, had been nothing but helpful. Hospitable bordering on nosy. But she seemed like a loyal and loving partner to my father so I decided I should give her some credit for that. "I left in a hurry. Sorry that it was such short notice for you." I said this as sincerely as my voice could project.

I had displaced my father to a cold floor. I'd forced them to spend too much for food. Yet I resisted the urge to feel defeated.

"If not tired, Kate, I drive you to the mall to buy clothes," Dad offered, just as how I remembered when he used to tell me on Friday nights that we could walk to a nearby store for an orange soda.

"Me too," Diday piped in. "I want the mall."

They started talking between themselves. At some point, my dad threw his hands up, which I could only assume was his way of expressing frustration. I understood some parts of what they said—that if Diday went with us, nobody would be left to take care of

Grandma. It started to sound like a heated argument with Diday articulating words like prison, boredom, sacrifice, all in two or three dramatic-sounding sentences, so I interrupted them by asking, "Is there somewhere I can easily just walk to so we can skip the mall?"

After our late lunch or perhaps early dinner, my dad apologized to me. "Sorry, Kate ha."

My heart started pounding as I turned toward him so that I could properly hear every word. I didn't expect this kind of talk to happen so soon.

"About what, Dad?" I smiled to encourage him to spill his words out.

He let out a sigh of regret. "I forgot to buy dessert. We are used to having the green mangoes as our dessert but this one we served was too sour. Here . . ." My dad handed me a spoon and peanut butter. "Do you remember we used to have this after every dinner?"

I laughed awkwardly. Half of myself felt disappointed while the other half wondered if my father would ever recognize how hurt I was when he abandoned me.

I shook my head and politely refused the peanut butter and the spoon. Unknown to him, I avoided peanut butter after he left. Years later, as if one of the cruel jokes in life, my son developed a fondness for it, so it became his ritual after almost every meal, or whenever he didn't get a proper sweet treat.

• • •

It ended with Diday taking me to a nearby dry market that sold clothes. "It's not a *passion* store ha," she cautioned me, mispronouncing the word *fashion*. "Because I shop at the mall."

I wanted to tell her that as long as there were other colors besides neon green, I'd be okay. Instead I told her, "I need a money changer." Diday was a little quiet so I explained more clearly. "I need to exchange my dollars to pesos."

"Ah, donchu' worry. Your papa tell I pay."

"Oh, please. I can't let you do that." I knew that I should not burden them any more than I already had.

"Ay, your papa tell I pay. Donchu' worry. Money, we have."

"Does dad have a job?"

"Businessman."

"Oh, what kind of business?" There was not a prayer I had recited that did not include my father and his welfare, so I was happy to hear more of how he managed to go through life all these years.

Diday had a habit of pressing her lips together in a chewing motion with her eyes quickly moving sideways as she pondered for the right word. "Do you know five-six?"

I found myself copying the exact mouth and eyes movement to demonstrate "I don't know."

"How about . . . hmm . . . sharks?"

"Loan sharks. Like money-lending business. Like that TV show."

"Yes, I know the TV show."

I wasn't exactly looking for confirmation on what sort of shows my dad's girlfriend watched on television, so I went on to clarify what information I wanted from her. "So, people borrow money from dad?"

"Just . . . hmm . . . neighbors."

With only dollars on me and no card machine at the market, I was left with no choice but to let her pay for my shopping. I was always frugal, but the current situation had left me penny-pinching stingy. Besides the lack of decent choices, I only grabbed the most practical, almost the same as saying the only option I had. I got two pairs of underwear and one porno-red underwire lace bra that was a total contradiction to the grandma panties. A plain white shirt and denim shorts, which were too tiny and snug, and made me worry that the panties, which were a little too big, would overhang.

The night was the worst. Diday explained that the mosquito net covering the bed was installed by my father to keep me safe from dengue fever. He had little faith in the thick layers of bug repellant he had insisted I spray on myself every two hours. I, on the other hand, had doubts anyone would be interested in being near me, even the bugs, with the strong, sour odor of the bug ointment. I was so repelled by my own scent and was so warm and sticky that I couldn't sleep. The net isolated us from everything, both the good and the bad—bugs, ease of movement, and breeze from the fan. Diday was similarly not used to the net, so she spent the whole night tossing and turning in discomfort.

Well, this is her bed, I told myself, *so I can't complain.*

I woke up with the worst combination of jetlag, lack of sleep, and overheating. I decided to call my mom in hopes that it might make me feel better.

"Where do you think I am?" I made myself sound chirpy and upbeat despite a throbbing headache.

"I already know, your *tatay* sent me a Messenger." The term "dad" had been relegated to my stepdad, Barry, so my real father was now a range of terms other than dad—papa, tatay, father. I was the only one who referred to him as dad. That was my choice as a daughter.

"I didn't know you're Facebook friends," I said teasingly.

"We're not. It's probably out of desperation. You must have worried him. You made us worry here. Kyle . . ." She paused, and I wondered if Kyle told her about the divorce. "He kept on checking with me on whether I'd heard from you."

"Does he know I'm here?"

"I told him as soon as I heard from your father."

"Did he say anything?"

"He asked if we have spoken."

"Please don't tell him I called so he doesn't think . . ." I hesitated for a second then said, "You know what . . . it's okay, Mom. Tell him whatever you want to say. Or whatever he needs to hear. Honestly, I'm really fine here. You can tell Kyle that."

"Barry can pay for your hotel if you don't want to stay with your father."

"Oh, no. I'm comfortable here." I said this as I swatted a mosquito on my leg. As soon as I ended the call with Mom, I proceeded to ask my dad for more of that spray.

The last thing I wanted was to trouble Mom with my grief. I thought it was best I ran away to suffer in secret. There was always bliss in not knowing.

CHAPTER 4

When You Became My World

"How true to our hearts was that beautiful sleeper
With smiles for the joyful, with tears for the weeper"
—John Greenleaf Whittier

California 2008

I t had been one heated summer. Not so much so for the relative humidity in the air, although the lack of moisture caused dry spells and short-fused moods, mine being one of them for sure. It didn't help that California wildfires had struck the state, with the Big Horn fire leading the lineup, then the nearby Gap fire in Goleta.

The warm season was almost over when I started suffering from random nausea. There were days when I was very lethargic and pallid. My mom must have noticed that I had not been eating well. "Unusually picky" was how she put it.

One morning, even before I got out of my room, I already sensed some activity in the kitchen. This was usually the case whenever my mom, on a whim, would decide to cook a big meal. As I walked into the kitchen, Mom looked my way and happily offered, "I can make you a plate now if you're ready to eat."

I went straight to the stove and said, "No, I can serve myself."

As I lifted the lid, the overpowering aroma of vinegar and garlic hit me as acidity unexpectedly thronged in my throat. I almost dropped the lid to the floor as I rushed to the bathroom. Chicken adobo was one of the dishes my mom cooked when I was growing up, so it was odd that the pungent scent made me sick to my stomach. When I returned to the dining table to join my mom, the look on her face launched a suspicion that we both could not easily verbalize—*I might be pregnant.*

I grew up in a traditional Filipino household. On weekends, my hair always smelled like garlic and burnt caramel as Sunday breakfast was a hefty serving of garlic fried rice with egg and cured sweet sausage. The Filipino bread rolls, *pandesal*, were the alternate light and easy choice, which we would dip into our coffee or warm chocolate drink.

When I was younger, whenever my mom prompted me to "eat some tasty," I knew what she meant. It was how she grew up calling the loaf of American-style sliced breads—tasty. After she married Barry, my white-haired, fair-skinned stepdad, I experienced what it felt like to have been adopted to a Caucasian household. My mom stopped calling the sliced Wonder bread "tasty." Our breakfast became oatmeal, fruit, and yogurt. We switched from deep-frying to baking. The beat-up old rice cooker was finally retired to the pantry. The kitchen started to bear a resemblance to Souplantation. And the house stopped smelling like garlic or vinegar. Until that morning when she decided to cook adobo again.

• • •

Kyle McDowell, on the other hand, was from a large family in a small town outside of Moab in Utah. He was third-youngest of the eight siblings. The McDowell household could be described perfectly in two words—systematic and utilitarian, at least in my opinion and based on the few stories Kyle had shared with me. The children were trained pragmatically, even at a young age. Kyle had recounted to me what it was like for him growing up. There was always food in the kitchen and his family ate together at precise times, the food spread out like a self-serve buffet. He made his own toast even when he could hardly reach for the counter where the bread, toaster, and homemade fruit jams were placed. That was why, in the beginning, whenever he came over for dinner to my mom's house, he was uncomfortable seated at the table while waiting for me to bring his plate of food, even though I reassured him I enjoyed doing this for him.

"I told you how it was for me growing up. Every little detail that I remember. You hardly shared any stories with me. You're not fair." I had been curious about his past.

"There's not much to tell. I'm not hiding anything. It was not sad. It was boring."

"Who was your first kiss?"

"She was a family friend. There were parties when we'd go to their house, or her family to our house. But I probably saw her only five times at most."

"Did you take her to the prom?"

"I didn't go to prom. We were home-schooled."

All the McDowell children were home-schooled. His persevering mom, ever the scholar, taught each child all the rudiments of life, including history, theology, music, Latin, math, English, and science.

"How about you? Who took you to prom?"

"Remember that guy I do errands for? Dropping off dinner for his mom? He was my prom date."

"He's lame."

"You don't even know the guy."

"He let you slip away. That's lame."

"Aww. That's sweet. Did they teach you that at home-school?"

"What?"

"How to sweet-talk a girl."

"Nope. Summer camp." He then gave away a laugh that I could only imagine carried some naughty memories with it.

The younger McDowell children were sent to month-long camps and the older siblings went off to paid internships during school breaks, so it made sense that his mom and dad were away themselves, on a cruise holiday.

Kyle grew up in a loving environment for the most part, but there were episodes when he felt neglected or invisible. He left home and enlisted with the US Navy as soon as he turned seventeen, just as his older brothers had. At twenty-four, Kyle had been living on his own for seven years. He was still subservient, but not to his family, just to the military.

• • •

The timing was not the greatest for us when I learned of my unplanned pregnancy. It was not unusual for Kyle and me to bicker over petty things. Like it or not, every fight paved the way for a more passionate squaring off. Unknowingly then, it was my hormones blowing me hot and cold that took us both to a heated argument and caused a temporary break-up.

When Kyle decidedly said, "Let's cool off," I knew then he was unwavering. It was not a big emotional outburst. He sounded calm, but out-and-out done with us. I was distraught, but it was not unexpected. It was a highly emotional time in which I failed to recognize the little being that was growing inside my body.

But pregnancy was actually the last thing I suspected. I assumed that the break-up was causing me to feel unwell. I was in the bathroom, holding a little white stick, waiting for miniscule lines to show. Lines that were life changing. Even more significant than those fate lines on our palms. When the test kit confirmed my mom's suspicion, it took all my guts and full disregard of pride to send Kyle the text.

We need to talk.

I lay in bed restless the night prior. With a slice of cold cucumber over each tired eye, I tried to restore some romantic sparks while I counted the hours until my date with Kyle. *Okay, it wasn't a date*—I needed a reality check.

I arrived first to avoid the lunch crowd and found a quiet spot for us. More fidgety than my usual self, like a cat on a hot tin roof, I sought comfort by browsing through photos saved on my phone. Thankfully, I had been less queasy the past few mornings, but the food cravings were way-out zany. We hadn't seen each other in weeks, and as Kyle approached our booth, he did a double take before placidly taking the seat across from me. What was that look for? Was it my breathtaking charm that he suddenly realized he missed? Or perhaps it was the way I eagerly gorged on the rice paper shrimp spring rolls and crispy coconut crusted tofu.

The two months that we had been separated suddenly felt like a lifetime with how different we both behaved toward each other, as if we had become strangers. Except for the curious look he gave me, it was hard reading Kyle—he was stony, a contradiction to his usual sunny vibe. If he was happy to hear from me, he didn't express it. There was no way to tell if he was still upset with me or if he had moved on and started to date again.

Kyle wore short stubble and tattered jeans. He looked great—the one thing that had not changed. I broke the cold welcome between us. "You look nice but a little different. Are you growing a beard?"

"I'd always kept it during weekends but started shaving it off when we got together. You complained about it, remember?"

"It really scraped my skin." I said this truthfully in my defense.

"To which I was just happy to do for you," was his counter, stoic and withdrawn.

"How have you been?"

"Same stuff. I'm still scheduled to deploy after the New Year."

I took that in bitterly. That was what started our argument—the separation that was about to hit us. I freaked out when Kyle told me he would be away for eight months. I said some hurtful things like "I'm not holding my breath waiting" and "I'm not ready for this long-distance set-up." Once I realized I'd put Kyle in a difficult predicament, I had already missed my chance to apologize. It was unreasonable to leave his job for me, or postpone his deployment as if it were just a vacation. I didn't know how to take my words back. I was so stern, even callous, when I said I was not cut out for that kind of relationship. But it was true at that time, and was still true now.

I tried moving past this to avoid another spat, but carelessly blurted out something that put us in an equally heated corner. "Are you seeing someone?"

"Why would you think that? Are you already seeing someone?"

Oh, how I missed polite, gentle Kyle. "It's just a random question."

"Everything is random to you. I don't toss things easily, Kate."

"Can you calm down for a second here, or I won't be able to say things."

"Like what things?" His tone was not a timbre lower.

"Like why I asked to see you . . ." There was a long pause. I was waiting for Kyle to probe me, implore me to say what I needed to share with him. He was not making it easy. He hardly looked at me. Tentative on Kyle's willingness to lend me a hand, I shared my pregnancy as casually as I could.

"I know we're no longer together. But you have the right to know. I'm pregnant with your child."

As soon as Kyle heard me, I saw his face turn pale. He was like the melted wax of an ivory candle—translucent while it was still warm, even hollow. What was he thinking? How was he taking the fresh news of this pregnancy? I watched Kyle like a lighted candle—could he be a flicker of hope or a scalding fire?

"Please say something."

It was as if my voice brought him back in. There was a positive shift to his stance. A smile slowly formed. He moved to my side and wrapped me in his arms.

Without hesitation, Kyle declared, "We should get married." His ice had melted, and the kind, soothing Kyle that I knew was back.

"Didn't you say that we're done?" I asked. The thing with me was that I always said things that were the total opposite of how I felt. A lame maneuver for self-preservation, to conceal my insecurities. Thankfully, Kyle was never about pride.

He took a long, deep breath, and locked his eyes with mine. "I'm sorry. The dumbest thing I ever said. Not anymore. We are more than good. We'll be a family."

"I didn't ask to meet you because I was asking to get back together."

There I go again, a little inner voice warned me. *I should shut up already.*

"Well, this is me asking you then." Kyle took my hand and said, "Kate, I want you in my bed. In my life. I am the father of your child. I want to marry you. We love each other, don't we?" He waited for confirmation, which I disappointedly failed to give. He then asked, "Will you marry me, Kate? Let me be a part of your life, our child's life."

The sincerity of his words and the doleful hazel eyes swept me off my feet once more.

It was not the first time Kyle was joining my family over dinner, but he was jittery just the same. He wanted to be the one to tell my mom and stepdad about our wedding plans. This dinner would ease my mom's worry about my unexpected pregnancy, despite the fact that neither of us had confronted the situation. When I told my mom that Kyle was coming over for dinner, she immediately left for the supermarket and came back hauling bags of groceries, as if she was catering for a big party.

Within two months, we were married. An unexpected, simple wedding of two people who met by chance and accidentally got pregnant. Be that as it may, every moment of that night was real.

When I was younger, I always thought that every bride marched to the altar to meet her groom accompanied by the song, "Here comes the bride, all dressed in white." But my wedding march was a somber piano solo. It was slow. I didn't realize how slow it was until I felt that it held me back from sprinting to the front. To my groom. That's how elated I was.

My mom insisted on a church wedding, which my stepdad was happy to pay for. We also had an elegant but not too overbearing reception. It was a modest celebration of our lovely but somewhat precipitous union. Kyle's big family took most of the short list of guests. By the time we cut and passed around the three-tiered carrot cake covered in white chocolate frosting, an amorous creation from my bakeshop boss, I knew everyone's name from the McDowells' side of the family.

The fall weather was perfect for an outdoor dinner, with sugar maples and russet autumn leaves scattered across the ground, masking the cement cracks and dirt, and adding a vibrant texture that complemented the warm yellow lights dangling loosely across the open space. The burning scent of pink pomelo grapefruit and bergamot competed with the sumptuous fragrance from the warm food being served on square plates. Kyle's parents opened the wine bar for everyone. I wore a classic satin pearl-white A-line dress designed to hide the baby bump, with a bustier top to highlight the pregnancy boobs. I kept my long black hair loose and straight, the way Kyle liked it. Witnessed by family and friends, Kyle took me to the center as we danced for the first time as a married couple. Kyle and I danced as if we were the only pair in the room. Our gaze darted to no one else but each other—the tips of our noses almost touching. My arms clinched around his neck as my fingers stroked his nape. His hands enfolded me closely. It was intimate and passionate. And our rhythms were coordinated.

More couples joined us on the dance floor. Mr. and Mrs. Richard McDowell, my in-laws, were the microcosm of papa bear and mama bear—affectionately warm, devoted, and altruistic. It was a marriage tested by time and eight kids. Whereas my parents, Mr. and Mrs. Barry Pepper, were the epitome of old-fashioned love and conservatism. They held each other as if they just met.

I was thankful for Kyle. It was in that moment that it hit me how blessed and somewhat dreamy our story had turned out. Who would have thought that an innocent mix-up of drinks in the darkest space of a theater would lead me to the arms of this sexy yet gentle guy? We made a dashing couple, young and very much in love. And nervous parents in due time.

After the wedding, once the out-of-state-family guests had left, things started to settle down, the way I imagined a marriage was supposed to. We had two months to ourselves before Kyle set off for his deployment to Kuwait. But time went by quickly, as it always did whenever you wanted to hold on to the moment. He was leaving right after the Christmas holiday, and wouldn't be home to see me give birth to our first child. My fears felt more apparent. Like a nose on a face, there was no way to avoid it. It felt like listening to water dripping out of a leaking tap. It was there, and I couldn't escape from the sound, the annoyance it was giving me, the torment of not being able to resolve it and save water. Except for the temporary separation, we were still grateful to have the holidays together. And the rest of our lives, of course, as we had promised one another.

Like most excited soon-to-be parents, Kyle and I spent the weekends shopping for baby stuff for our unborn child. Practicality was almost out the window as we impulsively bought what we deemed important.

"That's a different kind of blue, right? Maybe we get that shirt too." Kyle grew up wearing hand-me-down clothes. He promised not to do the same thing for any of his children.

I protested. I offered some sense to this insane shopping spree. "It's good practice if we only have three or fewer, but I don't know how we'll manage with a bigger family than that."

Kyle responded, "I'll just tie your tubes myself if we need to."

I zoomed a pointed look at him as if saying "that's not funny," but he quickly went in for a light smack that stopped any words of protest from coming out of my mouth.

As it did for most newlyweds, the honeymoon entailed long hours of cuddles and lazy lounges in bed, ardent sex any given time of the day, in every corner and in every creative way. It was still us. We'd always been this crazy about each other, emotionally and sexually. The difference was the certainty and confidence about our future, that we were in this for keeps.

But life was not always a bed of roses, I knew this even as a child. Winter was about to take this man to the desert. Perhaps it was the pregnancy hormones, the separation anxiety, or the agitation of a newly married wife about to face childbirth alone, but saying good-bye to this man was the toughest thing I ever had to go through, at least thus far.

I watched Kyle tie up the laces of his boots and put on his uniform hat. It was one cold morning, perhaps the coldest of that winter. As we moved closer to the door, chills went up my spine, competing with the overpowering fears that had kept me almost frozen.

"Will you please take extra care of yourself and our son?" Kyle whispered these parting words as he let go of my nervous embrace. "You have to promise me."

My body quivered bitingly as my knees got wobblier, betraying my fragile state. I watched Kyle hop to the work van to shuttle him away. He looked back one last time, his loving gaze stabbing my chest and causing me to gasp for breath.

I was like a flat tire when Kyle left. I was out of air. I couldn't function. I was stuck. I was a big belly running on a flat tire. I was a wreck for an unhealthy period of time. I had never allowed myself to succumb to misery until now. When you grow up alone, with a single mom who works tirelessly and is hardly home, and with no siblings or friends, you don't wallow in pain. There was nobody to console me. Despair was simply something I had avoided, even when my parents had separated and my dad went back to Manila for good, or as I watched Mom marry my stepdad.

My saving grace was the life in my womb. It saved me from a complete downward spiral. I couldn't wait for the days to come—to bring my child to this world and embrace him in my arms. And together wait for his father to come back to us.

Days were shorter as the sunset had been coming earlier than dinner and the nights became longer and lonelier. The mood swings were tolerable for the most part. The heaviness around my pelvis was more bearable compared to the heavy weight on my shoulder as I started to resent Kyle for making me miss him the way that I did. As much as he could, he would call and email. There were times when he would give me warnings without revealing much detail, "I won't be able to call for a few days, just letting you know so you don't worry."

Whenever I was home, I turned the TV on and kept it on just so I could hear another voice talking.

I was approaching the thirty-seventh week of the pregnancy when I got the phone call that Kyle was hurt. I didn't remember much from that call except the loud ringing that startled me, the spinning, light-headed effect it gave me, the stranger's voice introducing himself from Kyle's work, and the information that Kyle had been in an accident—*oh Kyle, my Kyle! What happened to you?* Most of the details escaped me. It put me in a dazed frenzy.

"He was briefly in critical condition." I think I heard him say that.

"Out of danger now." I was almost certain I heard that too.

"He'll call once he's cleared. After his debriefing." What does this mean? Clear of danger? So was he okay?

"He will be home soon, Mrs. McDowell."

I persevered on this promise. The ensuing hours turned into nerve-wracking days as I waited for another call. It was torture to be left in the dark—to know things but not completely know the details. *How come I have not heard from Kyle yet? Can he not talk? They said he was out of danger. What does that mean, exactly? Are they withholding information from me because I am pregnant? Christ, I need to know! I deserve to know. I can handle it. But maybe not. I don't know. Do I really want to know? What if it harms my baby?*

Severe anxiety welled up inside me, bringing me into labor earlier than expected. In slow but increasingly stronger waves, I felt woozy, perhaps from the pointless worries I subjected myself to. Toward the end of the day when the pain had become unbearable, I called my mom.

"I think I am spotting, Mommy!" Even when I was about to become a mother myself, I sounded like a child.

"Calm down. Take it easy. We'll be there soon to take care of you. Don't worry. You'll be fine."

I kept telling myself I would be fine. *I'll be fine. I'll be fine. I'll be fine.* It was a mantra for an apprehensive wife worried sick as to what kind of accident her husband was involved in, a mantra for a terrified mother unreasonably negligent for herself and her unborn child.

I was wheeled in on a chair by my stepdad while my mom, with disheveled hair and frantic eyes, held my hand and the maternity bag. The hospital hallway was too glaring with its shiny white floor and bright white lights that made me almost forget it was past two in the morning when I roused my mom from her sleep. I struggled between the joyful anticipation of bringing my son into this world and the dreadful anticipation for more news about Kyle.

My water broke just when I was checking into the hospital room, the agonizing contractions naturally progressing some hours after.

"Come on, Kate. You're doing good. Push some more."

"I can't. I don't know how. My jaws are locking. I . . . am . . ."

It was such a rapid breathing, so fast that I wanted to faint, like I could never catch my own breath. My jaws tightened. Cold sweat dripped off my forehead. Tears were running down my burning cheeks. I had a runny nose, which made it even harder to breathe, so I was using my mouth. I was huffing and puffing less as I was starting to feel numb. The spasms that had shortened my breath took most of my energy. And with all the chunks of unfamiliarity loosening at every stage of my labor, Kyle had been a constant sobering thought. Every ounce of my being clamored for him. There was not a single thing 1 wouldn't do or give up just to have him hold my hand right that moment.

"Kyle! Kyle!" I kept sobbing. "I want Kyle!"

Kyle was my world. Until I held my newborn sweet child for the first time. Not that the love for my husband had diminished. My heart just grew bigger, enough to hold them both. My son, bundled in a blanket as the nurse placed him in my arms, became where the sun rises and sets. He became my everything from that point on.

CHAPTER 5

When the Oyster Had Two Pearls

"No grit, no pearl."

—Unknown

had patchy mental images of my childhood in the Philippines. Glimpses of fun games like *patintero*—imagine intermixing tag and hopscotch—or Chinese garter, using long, stretchy garters, instead of jump ropes or a gymnast bar, while doing round-offs, and cartwheels, to get across the other side of the garter. I had cravings for *taho* for so long, our version of yogurt. Only it's warm and with boba pearls. I was proud of myself for having a lot of friends in the neighborhood and being one of the popular students in class. I was sociable. Confident. I spoke *Tag-lish*, Tagalog and English combined. Not because I needed to, but because it sounded smart and affluent.

When we moved to California, we had no friends or family to lean on. It was pretty much just the three of us. My mom had some friends from work, but she preferred putting her feet up during her days off, rather than socializing. Middle school was a big transition for most kids, but even more so for an immigrant child. Luckily, the kids were not as mean as those portrayed in TV sitcoms. Advantageously, there were many more like me in school, a whole assortment of scared, working-class, brown-skinned and dark-haired ESL students. English as a Second Language wasn't the hardest class—it even bored me. The toughest was US History. The only dead American I knew then was General Douglas MacArthur.

We were the stereotype of an immigrant family. Excited for opportunities while terrified of the monumental process of betterment that we had embarked on. We saved every penny we possibly could. Eating out, even at McDonald's, was a luxury. Our dishwasher served as a storage rack, too impractical to run. Paychecks were just enough to last until the next. I was the very definition of bilingual. I spoke English in school and kept my native tongue at home. I was the quintessential immigrant—conforming for legal and practical reasons while keeping my heritage.

I was closer to my dad when I was growing up, particularly during the first two years after our arrival in California. My mom was too busy putting food on the table to spend much quality time with me. It was more practical for my dad to stay home than for my parents to pay for childcare. My dad and I were big on TV dinner meals. This was usually on Fridays and Saturdays, when we wanted a break from eating fried tilapia or Spam, and was sort of the highlight of our week. My father was not very skilled in the kitchen. Whenever my mom had extra time to cook, that one dish would be our dinner for days, until the leftovers were gone.

When my father left us for good, different emotions started engulfing me. Guilt. Disloyalty. A greater fear than I had ever felt. Inside our small apartment, I heard their conversations that led to arguments. I was not in the same room when those happened, but it was a tiny space with thin walls. Therefore, I was in the midst of it all. It may have seemed like I took my mom's side when, by default, I ended up staying with her, enduring life in California. Nobody asked me what I would have preferred. I resented them for making that decision for me. But I couldn't hate my mom. I saw how she worked her ass off. She did the best she could. It was easier to resent Dad—he was the one that had left.

Eventually, the resentment became indifference. Perhaps I hurled it into my subconscious. One thing true then, even now, was that I was overridden with guilt. There was a part of me that couldn't forgive myself for almost deleting my dad from my life. I was my father's daughter, yet it seemed that I completely took my mom's side.

My mother, before she became Mrs. Adora Pepper, devoted her waking hours to me and her two hospital jobs. She was the complete opposite of Diday, who seemed to be a lady of leisure. Despite her petite frame and soft facial features, Mom was a tough cookie inside. Whereas Diday seemed to be brittle on the outside but was likely the opposite within, comparable to a half-baked cookie that would crumble easily when pressed on. Mom was very soft-spoken and nurturing, quite a contrast to Diday, who I was now learning was rather loud and bossy. Mom used to have easy wash-and-wear straight dark hair just above her shoulders. When she quit work, she had more time to take care of herself. She altered between short or medium length but always with sassy layers like Jane Fonda's. In more ways than mere hairstyle, she became Jane-like. Adora was a classic to Diday's maverick.

When I went to the kitchen to help out, I watched Diday sloppily chop a red onion. She discarded almost three thick layers of the bulb without much care, tossing them into the trash as if they were mere skin. One of the many things I loved about my mom was how she was never wasteful or imprudent. Onions were cut evenly and only the crimson tunic layers would go to waste. Every bit of the onion went to her dish, as if it was the most expensive ingredient on hand.

Later that day, I watched Diday spend hours on a phone call. With one leg folded and propped up on her seat, she flicked pieces of dead skin off her toes with her free hand. Then she switched the phone to her other ear to let up on the seared side. She also swapped the positions of her legs to continue the purging of her hardened calluses. At the end of the call, the evidence of how much time she had spent gossiping on the phone was speckled by the amount of dead skin on the floor. My mom, on the other hand, was always brief with her phone calls. And as sure as the sun will rise every morning, I also knew that my mother would never trim her calluses in front of anyone. My mom spent her free time at her garden, with her pink gloves and big straw hat on, sunblock on her skin, as she pruned the roses. The only kind of trimming you'd ever catch her doing.

My mom's nurturing characteristics were partly due to her job as a nurse. It was at work where she met Barry, who was there recuperating from a heart bypass. The hospital had repaired his heart, then Barry repaired my mom's. He was a good provider, something my mom never had in her life. She was a working student, then a wife to a househusband, then a single working mom. She had been working all her life, even at a young age before it was legally allowed. Until she became Mrs. Pepper, and finally enjoyed a nice retirement.

• • •

Diday finally agreed to take me to a money changer. It was not much cash but at least I could chip in on some food expenses. It had been three days of freebies.

"Do you still think of me as your father? Then don't worry about food."

Still, I wanted to at least buy them lunch. Although a week's worth of groceries would be more fitting. As we walked back home, Diday and I chitchatted about senseless things she or I was curious of.

"Do you see Hollywood from where you live?"

"The sign? Or the movie stars?"

"Both."

"Not every day. Not even often. I live one hour from LA."

"Ahh . . ." Diday proceeded to drill me. "Do you eat pissa every day?"

"Pizza? No. Not if I can help it." It was my turn to be curious. "Do you eat rice every day?"

"Ha, I don't like anymore but cannot help it."

"I remember eating rice for breakfast, lunch, and dinner, unless I was in school. I missed that."

"No, pissa is better."

"Oh, no. Probably not."

Just then, Diday tripped on something that almost set her to fall forward, but I was able to grab her arm. She also managed to stomp her now-bare foot for needed equilibrium. It would take a lot to topple this woman.

"*Pucha.*" Slang for "bitch," that was a word I recognized.

"What happened?" I asked while I watched Diday trace her steps back to pick up her other pair of slippers.

"Shit! My step-in."

"What? Did you step on poop?" Disgust must have been written all over my face.

"What?" Diday expressed in an even louder confusion. "Where's the poop?" She started to look around too. She was equally disgusted.

"Wait. Didn't you say you stepped in shit?"

Diday and I were in tears from too much laughing as she explained how she meant slippers when she said "step-in." We were both in a light mood as we made our way to a small shack that sold snacks. There was a menu posted on one wall—ice *buko* or coconut popsicle, cold *gulaman* which was a sugary drink with square jelly, *halo-halo,* crushed ice with milk, sweet beans, and jackfruit, topped with a sliver of flan and a scoop of ice cream.

We took the only table in the store and waited for our halo-halo. Even in the warm weather, the crushed ice did not easily melt, so I struggled to thump my spoon into the hardened chunk at the bottom of the glass. I decided to proceed with enjoying the soft toppings instead.

"When I was younger, I preferred chocolate over vanilla. But my son, oh my son, he was such a messy eater." I shook my head as I recounted. "So, I stopped buying dark-colored flavors because it was hard getting rid of the stains on his shirt . . . on the walls." I straightened my back and hurriedly scooped a small serving into my mouth. I caught myself sharing stories in my head out loud so I instinctively pressed my lips more tightly together, even when there was still food in my mouth. But Diday seemed more curious with how I ate the halo-halo.

When Diday saw that I started eating the jackfruits, the flan, and the beans before mixing all the toppings with the milk and the ice cream, she interrupted. "No, no. Not like that."

"Why?"

"Because later . . . hmm . . . when finished, but not yet finish, you'll only have ice."

"But it's hard to crush."

"You do this." Diday held the spoon like a knife and stabbed the hard chunks of ice repeatedly. She was a vision of ferocity, an image that I wanted erased in my head.

"By the way, there's something I wanted to ask you. Why did you say that the old lady upstairs is my grandma?"

Diday hesitated on this, then casually said, "Because it's correct. She is your grandma."

"How?"

"Your mama's mama."

"Biological? She's the sister of Aunt Puring, who raised my mom?"

"Yes. My mom's sister is *Auntie* Puring," Diday clarified. I even heard a hint of elation in her voice.

"Hold off. Did you say your mom's sister?" As far as I could recall, it was just two sisters—Mom's biological mother and Aunt Puring. I looked at Diday and started seeing the resemblance, as if the puzzle had just been pieced together, or like a secret that was finally revealed.

"You and my mom have the same mother?" I said faintly, the way one would for an embarrassing secret, mindful to avoid anyone hearing.

Diday became tongue-tied. Her eyeballs moved sideways too many times. She avoided my stare and the question by swallowing the biggest block of ice one could possibly fit into the mouth. Granted, there had been occasional confusions and miscommunications between us, but not this time. I had heard her and understood what she meant. Her sudden silence validated it. I decided to ask my father for more information later, instead of pressing on Diday. I had lost my appetite for the halo-halo. I stopped eating as soon as we stopped talking. Diday tried to buy time. She finished the tall glass up to the last drop of milk and by then, melted ice. The walk home was quiet.

And just when I was beginning to like her.

Dad sensed that something had gone wrong when we entered the house. He asked Diday, "What did you do to my child?"

Diday was teary-eyed, so I started to talk.

"Diday, can I have a moment with my dad?" This was the only time I saw Diday happy to be left out of the conversation.

"Dad, who's the woman in the second bedroom upstairs?"

My father was unable to answer me at first. But his expression was all that I needed to see. That look again. Twenty years ago. On my father's face. Worry. Fear. Remorse. A look that showed how he was begging for forgiveness.

Diday was my mother's half-sister. A sibling she never even knew she had. From a mother who gave her up. Mom's only surviving family, who'd searched high and low for her. By then, she was already in California. Alas, they found Dad. He took them in. They were his wife's family, after all. Adora's biological mom. Adora's half-sister. Adora's biggest torment, if she found out.

• • •

A thing of beauty such as a pearl was a consequence of intrusion into the oyster. When foreign substances like grains of sands seeped into the shell, oysters, as a natural reaction, produced a substance that covered the irritant elements, in the process creating a pearl. Romantics claimed that a pearl was the oyster's tear. To romanticize it further, producing a pearl was the emotional release of an oyster. Therefore, I could argue that the pearl was the oyster's catharsis.

Catharsis, to some, meant a positive outcome after a distressing experience, however traumatic. In simpler terms, it meant finding closure and a sense of peace.

"I need to leave this place," I said. "I think I need to stay away from you for good." They were short but sharp verdicts I managed to throw at my father before I stormed upstairs.

Dad tried to stop me and begged for me to stay. I couldn't. I felt I needed to choose sides again—and I didn't want to risk hurting my mom. Staying here implied I didn't take offense to my dad's romantic entanglement with Mom's half-sister.

"I don't hate him. I don't. I can't anymore." I said this as if trying to convince myself while I started gathering my clothes. I stopped for a second as I felt my knees shaking and sat on the bed to catch my raging thoughts.

I realized that there was too much sadness in me and I couldn't fit any more hatred in my miserable heart. One thing I knew I should do was start forgiving myself for taking my mom's side all this time—this was my catharsis. This was my purging moment.

CHAPTER 6

When Morning Has Broken

"The star grew pale and hid her face
In a bit of floating cloud like lace."

—Sara Teasdale

California 2009

I slipped in and out of my bearings. I was partially aware of the things encasing me at the hospital. A few times, I propelled myself to be sentient whenever I heard my son crying, or when he tried to latch on to me. For the most part, I had no strength. I felt like I was in a roundabout, my mind in foggy circles. I was numb. There were mumbling sounds, squeaky footsteps, a hushed paging system. And my stepdad's croaky voice. There were flashes of Mom stroking my hand. Sniffles. Light laughter. Phone beeping. Ringing. Kate. Kate. Can you talk, Kate?

For a day and a half, I was in a blank cold space. Medically, I was fine. Emotionally, it was slow progress. I was lost.

My mom must have said these words over and over to me. "Kyle called but you were sleeping."

"Kyle called again."

"Kyle left you a message."

When her words finally made sense—Kyle was able to call, therefore he was okay—I then became okay.

I was floored with emotions when I finally heard his voice.

"Baby, how are you feeling? Please take care of yourself and our son. Please do not worry about me. I am fine."

In between sobs, I rammed my words through to say, "I missed you. But I hate it that you are not here. I hate it more that you got hurt. Are you really okay?"

"I missed you so much, babe. I'm coming home soon."

"You promise?"

"Yes, promise. Wait for me. I can't wait to touch you. To meet our son." I felt him pausing to swallow a lump of anxiety. Kyle would do this whenever he was feeling something strongly—he would ease off to a halt to catch his bearings. He took a deep breath. "I have a name for him—William. Do you like it?" Pause. Deep breath again.

"Yes, of course." I attempted to sound encouraging. "Anything you want, Kyle."

"Sorry to make you worry. I can't wait to be home. Do you miss me? Because I've missed you so much."

"Yes, I miss you. When are you coming home?"

• • •

My mom couldn't agree more with people who said that words have healing powers. "You can stop treating her. She's okay now. All she needed was a phone call from her husband," she jokingly said to the nurse.

I found myself again. Mornings had a purpose again.

The thing about goodbyes and separations—whether by choice like mutual break-ups, by virtue of natural progression when children leave home, or due to cruel circumstances like death—pain is imminent and healing is a decision. Have you ever watched military children run after their dads or moms in an attempt to stop them from leaving? For most of them, this was the only life they knew. No different from a child of divorce, worried sick over an uncertain future. Both circumstances were similar, like looking at the same tree but during different seasons. In time, they get used to goodbyes and separations.

• • •

California mornings were still chilly and foggy. My son came home with me. He was always wrapped in my arms and provided me with some warmth against the cool mist. Harvest gave a sunbeam of hope, with roadside fruit vendors lined up along the roads. Residents saw more foot traffic at the Ventura harbor as whale-watching was again in season. Plenty of migrating birds passed through in the spring. Their chirping was a lullaby to a quiet household.

Willy was almost two months old before he met his dad. I was seated in this cold, hard chair in a dingy waiting room adjacent to a military airstrip, in the midst of a few other anxious families.

When the chartered 737 aircraft arrived, my heart pounded like a drum roll. The sound of the aircraft was what woke up my son, who was huddled near my chest. Not the murmur of good vibes in the air. Willy started to cry. Louder than he had ever done. My mom offered to take Willy but I refused it. I had waited for this moment—to wrap my arms around Kyle as we cuddled our son between us.

Kyle arrived in a wheelchair. We welcomed him with happy tears and wide smiles. And the howling cry of a baby. It was a temporary leg paralysis that was completely reversible with rigid rehabilitation and willpower.

"He will walk again, and it doesn't take a miracle to do that." Kyle and I had held on to this, what the doctor had promised.

Miracles were never impossible feats. They were everyday occurrences, big and small. Kyle and I treated each passing day with great expectations and hope. Over the course of time, things fell into place.

Kyle watched his son lift his head from his chest for the first time. In return, I watched Kyle lift his legs with more ease.

Kyle held Willy as our fragile son taught himself to sit on his own. I watched Kyle get out of the wheelchair, using the crutches for support.

For lack of a more beautiful word, it was a miracle watching father and son finally learning how to walk.

It was the kind of summer when the peaches and mangoes were more sugary-sweet than ever. Kyle came back home to us. When fall came, the stone fruits ebbed and were replaced by vibrant pumpkins. It was the kind of winter when the breeze was really strong, and my hands and feet were always cold, but we were spared from any storm. And by the following spring, our son turned a year old. Both father and son were walking. They were the wonderful things that happened in a span of one year.

The large backyard was laid out with playful picnic blankets and big cushions all around the grassy area. First-time grandparents, Mom and Barry, hosted Willy's first birthday party at their house. We decorated their yard with dangling red paper lanterns and sapphire blue balloons all around the open space. We cleared the right corner and arranged all the party cupcakes, red and blue macaroons, strawberry shortcake parfaits, red slushies and blue lemonade on a rectangle table draped in a white-and-navy gingham pattern. We stationed the food—a buffet of finger foods from pork pot stickers to spring rolls, buffalo wings to toasted shrimp samosas, and an array of meat, veggies, and cheese skewers—all on a matching table, in the opposite corner. At the center wall was a white projector screen that continuously played animated movies. We played fun music and games. We were surrounded by friends. Everyone was there to celebrate Willy's first year of life. And we all raised our glasses to Kyle for his journey to a fast recovery. When everyone sang "Happy Birthday," I started to choke because the words never felt more real. It was a happy birth and rebirth.

● ● ●

I squeezed the plastic bottle till the last drop of lotion landed on my palm. I lathered my arms, then proceeded to rub my neck. Kyle moved closer to me and proceeded to place his hands on my neck, so I let him continue with the massage. "Are you tired?" Kyle would often ask me, but I never complained. Willy, like most toddlers, was a handful. Kyle and I decided that one child was enough. I willingly quit work to raise our son. I was delighted to do this, even when times were hard. One morning, my mouth dropped as I saw a box of cereal tossed on the floor. I gladly cleaned up the mess. He was two and too young for a time-out. When Willy used a marinara sauce to add color to the white wall, I called it art before wiping it off. Whenever I stubbed my foot with the toys on the floor, I was happy it was my foot that got hurt, not his. Willy was a budding athlete. When he realized running was more fun than walking, I was thankful for the outlet for his energy. Once Kyle was home from work, he eagerly took over the watch. We took turns with the bedtime reading.

One quiet night, Kyle mumbled what could be perceived as silly for an outsider. "How could we possibly have another child? Do you think it would be possible to love a second child as much as we love Willy?" Kyle often asked me. I wondered this too but never said it aloud.

A lot of times we let him stay with us in our bed, except when we needed it to ourselves, the daddy-and-mommy time as we called it. We still waited for him to fall deep in sleep before we moved him to his room. Our world revolved around our son.

• • •

"Stop making him run so fast. Look at the bruises that have been showing up." I had started noticing some bruises here and there. I warned Kyle not to be too rough on his son.

"Don't worry. We'll be careful," Kyle reassured me.

Whenever our son said, "Em tire," Kyle and I, jokingly, let out a sigh of relief. "Finally," we would say, as it could be really tiring keeping up with his toddler energy.

• • •

Kyle was away for two weeks for work when Willy got sick. I consulted with his doctor over the phone, as it didn't seem serious enough to warrant a visit.

"His temperature has been a little over a hundred for at least twenty-four hours now. He seems to be struggling with his breathing."

"Does he have a cough?"

"Yeah, he has a cough." I suspected that it was the cough that was causing his fever.

"Just keep him hydrated. Plenty of fluids. Sponge-bathe him if he's too warm. Don't bundle him up too much."

The house reeked of maple and bacon as I prepared breakfast. Willy had not been eating well, perhaps due to his congestion. Because it had worked without fail in times past, I thought that this favorite food would lure his appetite. Willy had been glued to his bed and movies, and I thought perhaps it was because he was sorely missing playtime with his dad. He had been in no mood to play for days now. I anticipated seeing his vigor come back once Kyle returned from his travel, but I was worried.

"Uh . . . oh . . . Am I in the right house?" Kyle greeted me with a tight hug and a spiraling "can't-wait-to-get-you-to-bed" kiss in the mouth. Our apartment was remarkably the opposite of disarray—toys were neatly stored in their hide-away cubes, the kitchen was spotless, and there were no lingering piles of dirty sippy cups or bowls and plates. Only the chirpy voice of Barney gave away a trace of a toddler dominating the house. Despite his low-grade fever, Willy seemed fine. The day started almost too perfectly. My child was not whiny inasmuch as he kept to himself and his purple dinosaur. I made Kyle's favorite carbonara using the remaining bacon. Frozen French bread rolls were heating in the oven, and the lingering aroma of smoked meat was now mixed with the whiff of parmesan cheese and warm yeast. Kyle was never used to this kind of ambience. It was usually the scent of fried food, chicken nuggets, and potatoes. The floor was usually sticky from spilled drinks, and cluttered with toy trains and picture books.

I was less collected both as a mother and an adult whenever Kyle was away for training and work travel. He was always a source of strength for me.

Kyle joined our son in the living room, in front of the TV. Soon after, I heard Kyle start spurting out promises of a train ride and a weekend visit to the zoo. As I watched both propelled next to each other, I realized more than ever that they were two of a kind. The dramatic colors of their eyes, pale skin turned honey blonde as the sun kissed their skin. The arrogance of their noses. The rowdy sound of snorting laughter. Just seeing them together was enough for my world to spin, and that world spun around them.

We planned for an early night for our son so that Kyle and I could have a nice adult evening to ourselves. Ever obliging, our son went to bed early. We moved him to his room. Kyle opened a bottle of red and we sat on our small porch enjoying the evening breeze and bleak skyline with hardly any stars. Date nights had been reduced to this—once a week and home-based. But we didn't mind. Being away for two weeks made his touches more suggestive, making me more responsive.

"I wish we had a big backyard," he murmured. "We could lay out naked under the moon while Willy is tucked away in his own bedroom suite."

I laughed. "He'd probably get potty trained faster if he had his own bathroom. That would be nice!"

"Babe, you missed the part where I said we're naked and fucking in the backyard."

"Oh, I just chose to ignore it. I want to finish this wine first."

"Come here, babe." Kyle motioned for me to sit on his lap.

"No." I said this with a little resistance. "We have all night for that."

Kyle was persistent. We managed to make it inside the house, but we didn't make it to our bedroom. Our clothes had been tossed on the living room floor. His mouth on my mouth. His fingers on my nipples. His other free hand stroking the wet lips between my thighs. Kyle arched me backward on the couch with my elbows and knees bracing his weight while he humped on me tenderly until his urges motioned him more briskly. Like any married couple, there would be nights when lovemaking was gentle, even predictable. But like in any routine, just as the moon cycled back to its full form and peaked, we got nights like this—hot and on their summit.

After we caught our breath, we picked up our clothes and put them back on. We straightened the couch, put the cork back on the half-empty French Malbec, cleared up the kitchen, and got ready for bed. As a habit, I checked on Willy one last time. We had started training Willy to sleep without any lights on, so I relied on the hallway bulb to provide that narrow gleam against his dimmed room. I snuck a kiss on his forehead and straightened his blanket. As I pulled away, my foot caught on something, so I flicked the switch of his table lamp on and gathered all the toys into a storage bin. I scanned the room for any more clutter on the floor. I trailed my gaze to his bed, then a last look at my sleeping son. Terror suddenly gripped me—there was blood on his nose.

CHAPTER 7

When Hope Perched in the Soul

"One self-denying deed, one word
That eased the heart of him who heard,
One glance most kind,
That fell like sunshine where it went—
Then you may count that day well spent."
—George Eliot

L iam always had that impulse to travel, as if he was in search of something. Not that he was a nomad, he was more like an ant—strong sense of smell and the tendency to hibernate. Traveling was his way of hibernating.

He often held a book during dinner outings, or whenever he was seated in public alone. The book he held, a hardcover of Shakespeare writings with commentaries, was a gift from his mother—she had given it to him when he expressed trouble with sleeping. Afraid that Liam would become hooked on sleep medication, she sent him all the mind-numbing books she could find. That particular one was the biggest Ambien pill of all. It was worth the effort to bring a book with him, to keep the appearance of intently reading—this always served as a smokescreen to keep people from engaging him in a chat.

From where he was seated in the airport dining area, Liam caught a glimpse of her long windswept black hair. There was not a glaring light or flagrant movement to nudge him in her direction. It just happened that way. Hers was a petite body, almost frail, aimlessly walking like a headless chicken as she went into the café. Liam hurriedly removed his stare, although she was too distracted to even notice him. His eyes returned to the caption of an old photo he used as a bookmark,

"Then the little kite's paper stirred at the sight. And trembling, he shook himself free for flight."

His meandering eyes went back and forth between the woman and his book. He took another quick look at her willowy frame, shrouded by a red cardigan that was almost as long as her ankle-length black leggings. The image of the lithe red fabric and her swaying hair stayed with Liam as he went back to reading,

"Is it possible that on so little acquaintance you should like her? That, but seeing, you should love her? And loving, woo? And wooing, she should grant? And you will persevere to enjoying her . . ." Liam was distracted now. He was finally digging Shakespeare.

He closed the book, folded his arms, and watched as she despondently realized that all tables were taken. She was no longer a headless chicken. Her fetching soft features held a yearning expression. She seemed familiar. Liam quickly looked away when she scanned the room. As he casually glanced back, their eyes met. He motioned his hand to invite her to take the free seat next to his. This was uncharacteristic of him. Seemingly without any qualms, she walked toward him. Liam caught a whiff of her floral scent even before she reached the table. She mouthed what appeared to be an expression of appreciation.

He watched every single move so that he wouldn't miss anything. She appeared to be in deep thought. Twice she jerked away from the spoon, possibly burning her tongue from the soup. Those were the instances she seemed to put away whatever conversation she was having in her head.

Liam didn't want her to notice that he could only read her words, not hear them. He had to shake off his nerves, so he stood to grab drinks.

Without a single word on his part, he sensed that things were becoming a little awkward. He was never shy in using his whiteboard app to illustrate his thoughts—until that moment. Even before he had completely lost his hearing, he had always been a quiet guy. His voice, demeanor—neutral bordering on zilch. But never this muted as he felt that moment. What was it about her that made him feel conquered?

His mind was racing as she continued to disengage herself from him. She seemed in a hurry to finish her noodles and beer, to leave him to the table. He knew he might never have this chance again. It had been a while since he heard in his head the frenzied beating of his heart. Reeling under pressure as she motioned to grab her bag, he was compelled to hold her back. In a way, it was the only thing he could do to seize the moment. The starkest words to describe himself—*I am Deaf.*

He explained to Kate that he was originally traveling to Tokyo but turned around at the airport due to bad weather, and that he hesitated to rebook his destination for Manila.

"We weren't even supposed to be on the same flight. I was not supposed to go to Manila." Liam wanted to share with Kate how he thought there could be more to this chance meeting, but he was not sure how to express it.

"What happened?" Kate inquired.

"I didn't want to get stuck inside my Tokyo hotel because of the typhoon, so I went from arrivals to departures."

"Have you been to Manila before?"

Her messages seemed to indicate that she felt more at ease, and he started to relax.

"First time."

Liam learned that Kate was born in the Philippines before she moved to California at the age of ten and had not been back since. He explained how he preferred traveling to foreign countries where English was not widely spoken—the language barrier allowed for hand gestures or Google translate instead of verbal communication. He thought that English was widely used in Manila. He read from travel guides that even street vendors spoke and understood English, so Liam had never considered it as a travel destination. "I never planned for a trip. It must have been fate when I finally did."

This rendered her speechless once more, and he realized he may have overstepped. She seemed to retreat again into her cove, back to introspection mode, so Liam sent this message. "I can read lips, not minds."

She let out what appeared to be a shy, or nervous, laugh.

His memory had betrayed him with the passing of time, as was the case for most people. But unlike hearing people, he could only rely on faded memories to reminisce. He could still recall the sound of hysteric out-of-control laughter. Or the swishing noise that the bristles made when brushed against teeth. The barking of a Boston terrier or the lowly howl of a newborn puppy. And a female voice. Kate was the first woman Liam ever asked what her speaking voice sounded like. It didn't matter to him if she sounded like Daisy Duck or SpongeBob. He was simply curious.

Kate felt mystifyingly familiar to Liam, but then she also seemed different from other women he had met in the past. Her smile carried some level of shyness, even sadness. Her motions projected thoughtfulness. Her skin, in its most natural color of earthy soil and red sun, was alluring. Her almond eyes, with lustrous dark irises almost too big for her tiny eyes, spoke to him the most. There was intensity and yearning to her gaze.

"What's the book about?" Instead of exchanging messages, Liam used an app and handed her his phone. But Kate couldn't walk and text so she held her hand to motion that they should stop walking. Then proceeded to cue her other hand in an open-and-closed-fist motion. Whatever Kate was trying to sign for Liam was lost on him. He didn't have the heart to tell her that what she was signing meant "milk," or the gesture of milking a cow. Liam smiled, suppressing a laugh.

Unsuccessful in whatever it was she wanted to convey, she went back to the phone and entered a reply. "It's about her life without him." That was her cryptic synopsis of the book she'd just purchased, and he couldn't help but try to read between the lines.

After walking in circles for some time, they found a corner near their assigned gate. He wanted to exchange more messages with her, but she fell asleep almost instantly. When she dropped her newly purchased book on the floor, it did not wake her up. Liam reached for it, grabbed a pen, and scribbled a few words on a page about midway into the book.

• • •

He was disappointed to not have another chance to spend time with Kate after they boarded the flight from Tokyo to Manila. Not even at the baggage claim area, where he hoped to bump into her again. At last he spotted her red cardigan as she approached the exit door. His eyes followed her like they would a trail of crumbs, as if that would give off some clues for this strange ending. Then and there, he felt his phone vibrate, prompting him to a new message. Then it made sense to him. She's married. Although he was disappointed, he understood her predicament.

When he checked in at the Makati Shangri-La Hotel, he scribbled a note for the front desk clerk to read. *If someone by the name of Kate comes looking for me, please give her my room number. You can't patch the call through because I am Deaf. But please take a number and a message. Thanks.*

• • •

August in Manila typically had about twenty-two days of rain out of the thirty-one. There would only be five hours of tropical scorching sun each day, making it a very wet time to visit. But the month was almost over. The typhoon that just left the country was now in Japan. It was perfect weather for a stroll. Liam was usually the wandering type, rain or shine, warm or cold. But he was not in any mood for a walk, feeling too restless to step out of his room. So he decided to skip dinner and retired for the night.

When he woke up a few hours later, at two in the morning, Liam drew the curtain open to survey the city. The street was still filled with cars and the sidewalks with people. The sky was indistinct, with only the faint, slender crescent that was the new moon. His burdened mood revived to some degree of hopeful. He decided to forget Kate for now and try to love this city he had never seen. It was time to release his expectations.

Still, his mind woke him up every other hour. Each time, he checked the hotel phone for a flickering red light and his cellphone for any notifications. None. There were always racing thoughts charging through his mind and he was used to that. It was not a disorder. It was a way to fill the void. The silence. And tonight, he couldn't seem to think of anyone else, no matter how hard he tried.

In what was a very brief flicker of time, Kate had gotten under his skin. It was as if she had built a fire under his passive nature. She ignited him, even with such basic things as the way her silky hand felt as she grabbed him to go to the bookstore. The way she mouthed indistinct words, how she curved her lips gently to release a soundless sound—whenever she forgot that he couldn't hear. And yet her words clung to Liam. There was no disconnect between them.

She had needed a table. Liam was happy to offer. A conversation to distract her from whatever it was that troubled her. And some laughter to stop a looming meltdown. Someone to walk with. And pass the time with. He'd been there for her, and if she never made an appearance again, at least he knew he had done that much for her.

He used to have someone. Julia, his high school sweetheart. They had basically grown up together. He was her lighthouse—she was the stereotypical clingy girlfriend, too dependent on her boyfriend. When Liam lost his hearing completely, he slowly turned into a miserable person. But no more miserable than Julia. At some point, when he was too wrapped up in himself, she did a one-eighty. While he sat back, feeling sorry for himself, she moved forward. He watched her grow up and become more, while he was headed for the opposite. Deteriorating, becoming less. He had to let her go.

She hated him for this, but he knew she'd thank him eventually. And eventually that's what happened. As he healed and realized his biggest regret, Julia already belonged to someone else.

By noon, he got up for a quick shower and left to wander the city. When he emerged from the elevator and worked his way out of the hotel, he gazed back to take a look at how grand the hotel lobby was. The two enormous staircases, the floor-to-ceiling windows, and the large chandelier were all hard to miss, but he did. Or rather, he half-saw everything around him, as if through a filter. It was Kate—she was there, stuck in his mind, quelling his ability to be fully present.

As soon as he exited the hotel, his skin was bathed in the searing sun. It was a common assumption that tropical weather made people more passionate, when the mighty sun hollered everyone to life. He liked that about this climate, except for the glaring fact that the sun had blinded him. "Great. I can't hear. And now I can hardly see."

Sometimes he had harsher words for himself, but today he was going to make an effort to go easy on himself and enjoy the new place he had stumbled upon.

At six foot, two inches, he was towering, at least among this set of locals. Unmindful pedestrians would suddenly take a second look at him, which he tried to ignore. This sort of thing made him uncomfortable.

There was nothing else to do but to keep walking, and eventually his body language must have become more comfortable, because people had stopped looking at him as much. He was not bothered by the obvious disparity between luxury and poverty. Progressive skyscrapers of residences and offices against the seeming neediness of the street peddlers and workers. Commuters jammed in traffic, and huddled inside poorly ventilated, overloaded buses that made those local small vehicles—jeepneys—seem snug. He'd seen worse. Far worse situations in other countries. He kept walking, sun still glaring his sight until the first plush mall, which he decidedly went into.

Liam had never liked crowded spaces where he could accidentally run into people. That included malls. He went into the first Filipino restaurant he found, a place by the name of *Cabalen*. He wanted to taste the local food. Things she grew up eating. He wanted to know her culture.

It was a casual dining place that served a buffet of dishes. The labels helped, except that some were also written in Filipino.

Crispy *kangkong* was a fried breaded large spinach.

The roasted pig was like a Hawaiian *kalua* pork.

Crispy crablets were something Liam decided to be too much of an adventure to eat.

Okoy was another fried dish. It was like fritters but with some sharp edges that almost made him choke. He tasted the sweetness of the yam and the distinctive flavors of the shrimp.

Beef *mechado* was the dish he enjoyed most. It was basically a beef stew.

Ginataang kuhol. Snail in coconut sauce. Liam moved on.

The mall was a big labyrinth. In ancient times, a labyrinth was meant to trap evil spirits—until it evolved into a place of meditation. It never ceased to amaze Liam how poorer countries have more extravagant malls. This mall in Manila was so huge that it was easy to get lost in, particularly if one was not in his right frame of mind. Or if what one was looking for was not in this labyrinth.

When Liam drifted back into the hotel, he went straight to the front desk. It was the same clerk that checked him in. She remembered Liam because she stopped midway through what appeared to be a standard greeting and instead bowed her head. Then she shook her head to mean there was no message for him. "Thank you." Liam proceeded to walk back to his room while saying under his breath, "Clearly, she remembered my note."

Liam spent the next two days restlessly spinning in his mind. He was less hopeful of ever meeting Kate again with the passing of each day. Perhaps it was time to leave before another storm pounded its way into the city.

CHAPTER 8

When the Hour Was Ripe

"The heart asks pleasure first. And then, excuse from pain;
And then, those little anodynes that deaden suffering."
—Emily Dickinson

At six in the evening, sunset in Manila was about to arrive. It was almost getting dark. To a certain extent, it was daunting to trek out at this hour, and even more so for someone who had not been out alone and who was unfamiliar with the city and clueless about where to go.

Once my knees felt more settled, I paced back and forth in the bedroom as I went back to gathering my things while trying to figure out my next step. I struggled with the thought that I was breaking my father's heart once more. In the same breath, he was also breaking mine. To continue staying here seemed like a betrayal to my mom. I couldn't turn a blind eye on this infidelity—perhaps not to my parents' dissolved marriage, but to the family. And to decency. Walking out of here would be best. But where would I go? I couldn't call my mom and take her up on that offer to pay for my hotel. She would suspect that something went wrong here.

A weak knock at the door broke the hush in the room. "Kate, can we talk?" I ignored it. Diday continued to prod me on whether there was a chance for us to talk, to hear her out. She was relentlessly tapping on the door, the force of her knocking seeming to grow. I rushed to change into the same clothes I had arrived in—the only decent outfit I owned.

Diday was still waiting outside as I opened the bedroom door. She was about to say something when I stepped forward to hug her—a tight embrace meant for her to feel my appreciative but crest-fallen heart. We both didn't say anything. We both knew it was a real goodbye. My dad was nowhere in sight downstairs. It was probably better this way. He was quick to surrender once again. He knew there was nothing he could say to convince me to stay. He had fig-ured out that much about me.

I walked one block to the same route that Diday and I treaded during our bonding moments. The street was even more crowded with people rushing to get to dinner, or home. Flickering, dimmed yellow lights were indicative of a sunset that had come to pass. My heart was pounding for many reasons, but primarily because I felt lost and scared stiff. I walked further until I found an empty cab.

"Where do you want to go?"

"Wait *po*." I hurriedly looked through my phone to the messages that Liam had sent. "Makati Shangri-La."

The cab driver acknowledged the destination with a nod of his head as he pushed a button to start the meter.

In truth, I had suspected that Liam and I might actually meet again. I had been re-reading our exchange of messages. A part of me had wondered if he had forgotten about me. He never replied after my last message. But I had expected just as much. I should have explained my situation at the onset instead of an abrupt text as I said goodbye. Nobody, and certainly not Liam, deserved to be brushed off, yet I had done just that to him.

• • •

When I arrived at the hotel, I was a little intimidated by how grand it was. I knew that I couldn't afford to stay here. Financially. Or even emotionally. Perhaps a night or two at most. I headed to the restaurant lobby and got myself a table. I needed time to think things through. I ordered the cheapest glass of local beer. Then I started to debate on what to tell Liam.

"Hi. It's Kate. Where are you?" Delete that.

"Hi. It's Kate. Are you still here in Manila?" Delete that too.

"Hi. It's Kate. How are things?" Delete that. I'll end up drunk and with a huge bill by the time I get to my point.

"Hi. It's Kate. I'm here at the hotel lobby. I need help." Sent.

• • •

The lounge was skirted by floor-to-ceiling glass windows overlooking the stillness of the evening. The local band played at a brisk tempo, trying to detach the patrons from the tranquility of the night to bring everyone to a heightened level of energy. The drumbeats were like vibrant confetti surging through the air. The guitar and the vocals gave off soothing sexiness to the verve. Until the music wound down to more subdued tones. One hour had already passed, and the musicians were winding down with what they had announced was the last song for the night. I was more than jittery. Why had he not replied? And then the thought crossed my mind—what if he'd met someone here? What if he had someone in his room now? What if he was really flying here to meet someone?

I covered my face with both hands. I wished the ground would just swallow me in. I felt awful. Maybe I had been really naïve to believe a word he said.

I watched passersby more intently. I paid more attention to couples. A man of his similar build, with a lady clasped to his elbow, turned around in my direction. I let out a sigh of relief when I realized it was not Liam.

In the beginning, I sipped my beer as if it was burning my tongue. Gingerly and prudently. A few tiny sips for every song—until my intake picked up along with the beat of the music. While I watched the band putting away their instruments, I knew my time was up. I had polished off my beer some time ago. The last drop was already too warm for my liking. I was now washing down my fretfulness with a gulp of cold water. I rubbed my forehead, and contemplated calling Mom for help. But I quickly put that option away. I should avoid Mom for as long as I could, or she would end up learning about Diday.

Please Liam, answer me.

"Would you like another glass of beer? Or perhaps something to eat?" A smile so convincing it almost sounded like it was out of genuine concern.

I knew it was past dinnertime. Like Liam, I could clearly hear the murmuring sound of my hunger within myself. "Not for now. Thanks. I'm actually waiting for someone." *Please leave me alone now.*

It had been two hours. The live band had been replaced by a solo pianist. The air was filled with conversations that overpowered the mellow harmonics. My phone battery was dangerously low. It might be harder to find an alternate solution if I waited frivolously here. Time for Plan B—except I didn't have one of those yet. For whatever reason—which only Liam knew—I hadn't received a reply so I paid my bill and got up from the table.

I was dragging my feet toward the exit door because part of me was still hoping to hear from Liam. Perhaps he had not seen my message. And because I didn't know where else to go. I wondered if I should I ask the valet where to go for a cheaper hotel—that seemed like my only option.

I was inches away from the open sliding glass door when I felt a force pull my hand. I looked back to find Liam. Out of breath. Shirt inside out. Hair disheveled with one side flattened against his head. Pillow creases on that same side of his face. Glassy eyes intently staring at me. Then a thoughtful beam, as he followed it by encasing me in the warmest embrace ever.

CHAPTER 9

When You Cried for the Moon

"A gaze blank and pitiless as the sun."

—William Butler Yeats

California 2014

"Willy, do you know what a tattletale is?" Dr. Jarvis, the pediatric oncologist, in her warmest voice, asked my son during one of her rounds.

"Yah, Rosie. She . . . ah . . . um . . . tada-tale!" I laughed softly at my son. The doctor had no idea that my son didn't have real-life friends, except the characters he watched on TV. Because I was a stay-at-home mom, my son had never set foot in a daycare. He was still too young for kindergarten. From time to time, we would get invited to birthday parties, but Willy didn't have a constant playmate, not even a cousin or a neighbor. This realization weighed heavily on my shoulders. *Don't worry, Willy*, I said to myself. *I'll find you a best friend as soon as we check out of here.*

"What made you say that?" Dr. Jarvis, like most of the attending physicians, engaged Willy in simple conversations. Perhaps to win his trust, or just be a friendly face in general. Thus far, Willy had managed to deal with all the pain, treatments and medicines, restrictions, and questions thrown at him like a champion.

We had been at a hospital in LA for over three months—our third confinement here. Previous stays had been much shorter. The nurses had become familiar, some I even befriended, or called by their first names. Tita Claire reminded me of my mom when she used to wear scrubs. And her merciless warnings to Kyle made Mom's reproaches seem like a cradlesong. "Be good to your wife and child. You better not fool around while you're home alone and they are here!"

I had only left twice since we checked in. Kyle, whenever he could, would drive up to join us after work. It was an hour commute each way, and that was without traffic, so it was hard for him, too. But whenever we needed him, he was here in a blink. As well as weekends.

"Rosie said . . . then . . . um . . . Caillou . . . um . . . I don't like Rosie," Willy said, reasoning out his thoughts. There were days when my son was more coherent and days when all we could hear were his whimpers due to discomfort.

"How so?" the doctor probed.

"Don't know. Am tired."

"Oh, no worries, Willy. I understand. I only asked because I wanted to tell you quickly that we also have cells in our body that are tattletales. They're important too. They tell on the bad guys, the viruses, the bacteria in our body that want to harm us. That's why little things that you feel—don't be shy to tell us. Or tell Mom. Sometimes the tattletale forgets to do their job."

It had been a very confusing "let's-see-how-his-body-will-respond" journey since we started suspecting there was more to his lingering fever and fatigue. We spent several weeks chasing for second and third—and better-in-general—medical opinions. The first time I heard leukemia, I wanted to storm out of that doctor's office. It felt like I was in a cold torture chamber that was crafted for the sole reason of tormenting mothers like me. Our fragile Willy went through a harrowing series of tests, including a bone marrow biopsy, to confirm what they all had suspected, and what I had been unwilling to accept— acute lymphoblastic leukemia.

"It may sound overwhelming. And it is. And I understand. But you have to put the fears to the side—we need to focus on his treatment plan. It is curable." Dr. Jarvis said this to me over and over.

Kyle had to tell me to stop fighting off the diagnosis. Again. And again.

"What if we go to Boston. I heard they have better hospitals. Maybe it's not leukemia. It doesn't seem like he is getting better."

"You have to trust the treatment plan, babe. They've monitored Willy for a while now. It's better to keep him here than start somewhere again and waste time figuring him out, like we're back to square one. It's not helping him when he knows you're also scared. We need to focus on his treatment, instead of chasing after whatever it is you prefer to hear."

"But they could be doing it wrong." I was worse than Willy—my irrational outburst was like that of a toddler when not getting the results I wanted.

Have you heard a mother lament about her sick child? It was no different from the petrified wailing of a lost girl begging for help. Willy's health ordeal was a big blow to our family. It was hard to witness our son go through all the physical discomforts and those rigid tests. The most heartbreaking part of it all was that we couldn't do much but just watch while our son had to experience all of it directly—the sharp pinch of the needles, the throbbing mouth sores, lingering headaches, back pain, chills, and the nasty effect of chemotherapy on his young body. Whenever Willy could not hold food in his system, I didn't take a bite of anything either.

Willy's hair started to fall off in clumps. Patchy bald spots had progressed all around his scalp. The doctor reassured us that it was a good sign, that it meant that the drugs were doing their job. One weekend, Kyle shaved off his head and then asked our son, "Hey buddy. Do you want to look like dad?"

Willy agreed to shave his head, to look like his dad. It was just hair after all. On a few occasions, I caught him stroking his head, conceivably feeling strange about this somewhat jarring change.

That same night I decided to tell my son about Rapunzel. "We don't have a book on this but I remember her story from when I was a little girl. Did I ever tell you about this princess and her long hair?"

Willy shook his head but his eyes widened to demonstrate his interest. "Well, her name is Rapunzel. She has beautiful long hair, but you will see why Mommy thinks the princess is better off without it. She lives alone in a tower with no stairs. She never leaves the tower and nobody can come up to visit her, except for the witch.

Rapunzel sends her long hair down so that the witch can use it to climb up."

I paused and checked on Willy. "Do you like it so far?" He moved his lips into a weak smile.

"One day, a prince watches how the witch is able to climb up the tower. He copies the witch and is able to meet Rapunzel. But the witch gets angry with Rapunzel for being friends with the prince. She cuts off Rapunzel's hair and sends her to the desert. The next day, the prince comes back to the tower, shouting 'Rapunzel, Rapunzel. Let down your hair.' To his surprise, it's the witch who's waiting at the top of the tower. The witch is really jealous and, yeah, evil. She pushes the prince off the tower and he lands on some thorns that pierce his eyes, so he becomes blind." I looked at Willy to see if he was still awake. "Does it make sense?"

Willy faintly nodded. "Mom, tell me more. The prince."

It was reassuring to hear that my son was more interested to hear about the prince. It warmed my heart to notice that he connected more with the bravery of the prince than with the burden that I worried he mourned over losing his hair. "Well, miracles always happen. Like magic in the storybooks. The prince heard Rapunzel's voice in the desert. They met again. Rapunzel's tears fell on his face, his eyes. Those tears healed him. He was able to see again. And they lived happily ever after."

Short of promising my son a miracle, I made a lot of promises to Willy whenever he was in a mood to talk or be social.

"I promise to take you to Disneyland as soon as your body is stronger." Willy gave me a weak smile.

"I promise that you won't miss trick-or-treat next year." Worried that he might have to wear this year's costume again as he only wore it while in bed, he asked if he would still get a new one. "Even better—Mommy will buy two costumes."

"I promise an afternoon of bike riding with a new friend."

"Frrrendd?" Willy was curious.

"I'll knock around the neighborhood asking moms if they have kids who can hang out with my handsome and healthy son."

"Nah girls." I chuckled at how he seemed annoyed about the idea of hanging out with a girl. I wondered what age he would be when he'd change his mind about girls.

"Em wanna kite, Mommy."

"Oh yeah. You and Dad tried that before. We read this book about kites, then you kept asking Dad to teach you how to fly one. We will do that again. I will tell Dad. I'm excited."

• • •

Willy had always loved books. Even before he could read, or even say a word. The colors must have lured his eyes. The smooth, glossy pages must have pacified his senses.

"Dad brought your kite book. Do you want me to read it to you?"

His eyes were already shut but he managed to mumble what I could only assume was a yes.

As I started to read his favorite lines from the book, my voice started to break. After almost every few words, I would stop to breathe in and out then look up at the grid tile ceiling, as if there was a proven science that would pull the lurking tears back in. I was grateful his eyes were already shut so he couldn't see me cry. I was careful so that my tone would not betray me. Almost to the finish line, I stopped to check on Willy. He seemed to be already asleep. I finished the poem more for myself. Every night, I had to remind myself to celebrate my son and his courage.

"They rested high in the quiet air, and only the birds and the clouds were there.

Oh, how happy I am! the little kite cried. And all because I was brave, and tried."

I wiped my tears away and placed the book back on the table. I walked the few steps to the door to switch off some of the lights illuminating the room. Then I went back to my chair and I watched what was for me, and probably for Willy, the best part of each day. It was the part where there was only his resting body—where no pain, or needles and doctors, could get to him.

• • •

Numbers are markers to illustrate progress. The changes in time. Eleven months for a tree to bear fruit. Ten months to build a house. Nine months to form a life in your womb. Thirteen months of treatment. But then there will always be that one day when nothing matters anymore, including time. One day—it was his kidney. Everything changed because of that one day. When everything happened so quickly, it was barely enough for us to catch our breath. But not my son. He was too worn out to catch his own.

The bond between a mother and her child is one of the strongest in nature. And for as long as she is alive, she will always be a mother to her child. I heard a grieving parent once say that there are words and labels to every occurrence expected in life. An "orphan" for a child losing a parent. "Widow" for a woman losing her husband. "Widower" for a man who's lost his wife. But to lose a child does not reflect the natural order—it is not how life was designed to happen—so we don't have a word for that.

Yet the hardest thing a parent can ever do is bury a child.

When someone said to me that my son was now a child of God in heaven, in my heart I knew that person had never lost a child. How could you tell that to a grieving mom? Only someone ignorant to the pain of caring for a sick child, only to lose him in the end, can imagine there to be comfort in those words. Heaven earned another angel. Fuck that! I watched my child—tired and beat by illness—abandon his last bit of strength. Surrender his young life to his creator's arms. I can't blame him. It was too much for his fragile body. He was just a child. Barely five.

It was the Fourth of July, 2014. 8:05 p.m. The hospital staff had removed our son, his lifeless body, from the room.

Take his body, I thought. *My son will always be in my heart. In my dreams. And waking hours.*

Kyle drew the curtain open as the fireworks started to light up the sky of Los Angeles, the city of angels. We both sat on the bed facing the window—his hand squeezing my hand, his eyes blood-blistered. His anger was expected. His loud wail was a stark contrast to my soft sobs.

The world took my son from me. I had nothing left to give, not even a howl. I was in so much pain. I was numb and with no willpower to move forward. To move at all.

The next couple of days were a blur. All of Kyle's big family came to town again. I had forgotten their names, but there was no cake to be served this time. Kyle had calmed down around his family. But that didn't mean he had recovered from our loss.

"I think I've gotten so many hugs so many times," I said, "that it's started to make me cringe whenever someone offers to hug me." I always lashed out with my complaints to Mom. My words had been bitter, particularly when she incessantly offered to console me—as if her comforting words would ever make a difference.

"But they mean no harm," she said. "Those offers of hugs were not to offend you. But to help you."

"What makes you think that could ever help me?"

"Well, one can only hope for it. You can't be angry at people who wanted to offer their condolences."

"I don't need their words. I don't need their hugs. The only hug I'll ever need is from one person. From my son. And he is dead. And nothing can ever bring him back to life. So people should just stop being generous with their hugs. As if they will ever matter to me." I was harshest to my mother. She was an easy target. But even with my toughest words, she gladly took in what I had to say.

• • •

There was one afternoon when the pain was beyond measure. I was crouched on my side. My back was curved, and my head bowed toward my knees, which were bent and drawn to my chest. I was like a curled-up fetus. Kyle came back from work and found me that way. He couldn't do much. He also slumped in bed, his face flat on the pillow to conceal a loud outburst.

We spent many nights just like the way we were at the hospital—he was still angry and crying loudly, while I had the same soft sobs. Our curtains were drawn open as we stared at the night sky, wishing for one of the stars to bring back our angel.

CHAPTER 10

When It Could Have Been Just Bread

"These are the days when birds come back,
A very few, a bird or two,
To take a backward look."

—Emily Dickinson

T he hotel lobby was like a stately arena, brimming with extravagance—except that there were no benches orbiting the room. But the hotel was still full of curious onlookers. Liam took the heavy tote bag from my shoulder and towed it to his. Without hesitation on either side, Liam held my hand as we walked toward the elevator. There was no reason to feel like it was a walk of shame, yet I felt paranoid, like someone about to get caught doing something illegal. Why did it seem like one of the desk clerks was looking intently at us? At me! I wondered if I was not the first woman Liam brought to his room. Well, I was here for a different purpose, and I had nothing to be ashamed of.

Liam was now looking at me more intently, perhaps trying to read my mind again. I reassured him with a smile, then shook my head to mean that whatever I was thinking was not important. Two more couples joined us in the elevator. Liam and I took one corner. It was one of those enclosed spaces where nobody wanted to make a sound or breathe too heavily. Liam seemed the most relaxed among the six of us. He was used to silent spaces. His hand still clutched mine.

I have to be perfectly clear that I'm not sleeping with him.

Once inside his hotel room, I sent a message. "Thank you for meeting me downstairs. I had nowhere else to go."

Liam's reply came instantaneously. "I'm happy to see you."

I noticed one king bed with one side unmade, and a loveseat. No signs of a lady friend or a second guest. I took a deep breath and then hesitantly asked, "Is it okay to bunk up here with you? I don't have much money to spend on hotels. I can stay on the floor or chair."

"You're welcome to stay as long as you need to. But I can't have you stay on the floor or chair. We'll share the bed. I promise not to touch you."

I looked straight at him and mouthed the words "Thank you." I was even more grateful that I didn't have to make that awful let-me-be-perfectly-clear speech.

"Let's have dinner first. What would you like? Room service? Japanese, or steak downstairs? Short walk to the mall?"

"You decide."

"Room service, then."

I watched Liam go to the room phone and punch in our dinner order. He then went to mirror his iPad with the television. He handed me a wireless keyboard connected to his laptop, while he used his iPad to type in a message. Our chat was now emitted on the TV screen. I then proceeded to shut off my phone. I saw no use for it for now.

He must have realized that my wardrobe was limited. It would have been impossible for him not to notice that I was wearing the same clothes when we met at the airport. "Do you want to borrow one of my shirts? You'll probably be more comfortable. But I don't have any bottoms I could share with you."

I laughed at this. His boxers might even be a better fit than the grandma panties from the market, but I was not about to share this. I nodded at him to accept his offer.

I excused myself to use the bathroom. "Oh my gosh." I let out a series of excited trills. *I miss hot showers. I'm so happy I could sing.*

And sing I did, as I took a luxurious shower. Fortunately, Liam couldn't hear my bad rendition of "I Will Survive."

After freshening up, I walked out from the bathroom a little self-conscious. His shirt was long enough to cover the grandma panties, but I'd have to be careful. I thought I might die if he were to bear witness to this horrendous underwear.

At the end of the room, next to the window, I was astonished to walk into a lovely dinner set-up. I had seen this once or twice in the movies when lovers ordered in. *No*, I had to remind myself, *this is not a romantic getaway. We are not in any romance. Fancy hotels always set up room service like this. Liam didn't do this on purpose.*

On a round table in white linen, covered by silver domes, were the mystery dinner dishes. When Liam had asked me what I wanted to eat, I had answered with "surprise me." And so he had—he had been strategic in ordering one American dish, a fabulous-looking classic hamburger, with parmesan truffle fries on the side, and one Filipino dish, *tinolang manok*, a chicken soup dish in ginger-flavored broth with green papaya and chayote wedges, bok choy, and spinach, with aromatic jasmine rice on the side. A small plate of oval custard topped with yellow mango cubes was next to a silver ice bucket that kept a bottle of Italian prosecco and two bottles of San Miguel Light beer chilled. We agreed to split both dishes.

"How do you like the soup?" Liam was on his iPad as he handed the keyboard to me.

"It tastes just like how my mom cooks it. Do you like it?"

"Yes. A little disappointed though. I thought the sparkling wine or beer would go well with it."

"Only water will taste good with soup."

"Not true at all," he responded.

"Tomorrow, I'll find a soup dish for you to try. You've not seen all the kinds of soup dishes they have here."

"Is it the pork blood dish or that sour soup with the fish head?"

My mouth was wide open in surprise. "Who have you been hanging out with?"

"Nobody. I went to this Filipino buffet twice and tried most of the local dishes."

"I'm impressed. I've missed all the food I grew up eating. When my mom married my stepdad, she stopped cooking them."

"Why didn't you learn to make them yourself? You must be a good cook."

My husband and son had shown no interest in the Filipino

dishes, but I was not about to share this, so I veered our talk away from that. "What makes you think I'm a good cook?"

"You have a few burn marks on your right hand."

Wow. He seemed to see everything in me, every little detail.

"Impressive." I winked as a natural reaction, without caution— and I hoped it didn't come across as flirtatious. He replied with a relaxed smile crossing his fine-looking face.

The silkiness of the coconut custard and the sweetness of the mango were such a nice treat. He had been nothing but gracious, from the thoughtful dinner and dessert, to taking me in without any caveat to the favors he gave me. A piece of bread would have sufficed.

There was not a dull moment with him, not a single lull in our conversation. It bewildered me that we'd had more conversations the few times we were together than I'd had with Kyle in the past few months. Perhaps he was simply friendly and chatty with everyone.

But I had to be honest with him and stop the casual talk. "I might have to cut this trip short," I told him. A messy shift to an already chaotic plan.

"Do you really want to go back to California so soon?" Liam gave me an earnest look.

"I don't know." I paused for a while because I really had no idea. I looked at the expression on his face, trying to figure out if he could read my life story. "When are you checking out here?"

"I'm supposed to leave in two days, but I don't mind staying longer to keep you company."

"Why?" It didn't exactly make sense to me why he would change his travel plans for someone he hardly knew, but I somehow believed that he would in fact do this for me.

"Why not?"

He caught my gaze but this time I didn't look away. I kept my eyes on his. Sometimes a stare can express much deeper things than spoken words. I understood his hunger for someone. I felt I could be that for him. I felt safe with him. I felt wanted.

With a heavy sigh, I offered the reality to Liam. "I'm married."

"I remember. The last thing you said to me." Then he added, "Is that why you're running away?"

"Probably one of the many reasons." I was not proud of the fact that I had run away, had avoided even thinking about it in those terms.

"Then you need longer than weeks."

I smiled but avoided his eyes, keeping my own focused on the letters on the keyboard. *Yup, I need a lifetime.*

Except for the prosecco, we were finished with everything laid on the table. He handed me a glass and offered a toast.

"Cheers to your kindness." I said this to myself, under my breath.

I swirled the wine glass aimlessly while deciding what to do next. I opened my mouth to speak and then quickly closed it. Once I was convinced that it wouldn't hurt to ask, I sent this onto the screen.

"How long can you extend then?"

He did not hesitate in responding, "How long do you need me to stay with you?"

"Let's find a cheaper hotel so I can split the cost with you."

Were we really staying together? It felt unreal.

"Kate, don't worry about it. Just tell me to rebook my flight and I will."

"My husband asked for a divorce, so I panicked and ran away." I paused and deliberated on the right way to say things. When Liam moved his hands to type a message, I held out my index finger to indicate that I had more to say. "My real dad, whom I was supposed to stay with while here, turned out to be a disappointment. Again." I paused, stealing a quick glance to see his reaction. He was intently looking at the television screen, as if digesting every word. I continued. "I don't know who else to turn to for help while here. But I'm in no position to ask you to change your plans for me." I placed the wireless keyboard on the table and waited for whatever Liam had to say.

"I like you, Kate." His sagging posture gave away his reluctance to admit this.

I took the keyboard back to my lap but found myself confused about what exactly to tell him—how to wrap up the complexity of it in a nutshell. "I'm still married." I felt defeated as I reminded him again.

"You've told me three times now." He looked my way with an I-heard-you-the-first-time smirk. It was not the arrogant kind. More like a compassionate and genuine sort that made me melt.

"How can you possibly say you like me? We don't know much about each other." My chest was pounding.

"Then give us a chance to get to know one another. At least a week. If you're ready to fly home then, we'll fly back together."

After a long back-and-forth in my head on what to do next, I sent this to the screen. "Can we just be friends for now?"

"I thought you'd never ask."

• • •

It was probably past midnight. Mid-afternoon in California. We were both in bed. I was on my side with my back turned away from him. I heard slight movement, perhaps his hand on the bedside table. Then a flicker to turn the room pitch black. I visualized him lying really close to the edge of the bed, much in the same way as I was. There were more images in my head that kept me awake whenever I shut my eyes—my son, my mom, my dad, my divorce—so I decided to stare blankly at the wall, at the darkness. Sleep seemed more elusive—more than it had during those nights being trapped inside a mosquito net.

There was light movement on the bed. He was probably on his back now. I also needed to switch sides, as my arm had started to get numb.

An hour or so had passed. No movement on either side. As still as the night. As expected of someone pretending to sleep.

Perhaps my mom was already worried sick about me. The one thing she had asked that I do was keep my phone on. Answer her text messages and calls.

I moved inconspicuously as my hand blindly combed the bedside table for my phone. The brightness from the screen slightly illuminated my corner when I pressed the on button, so I hastily tucked the device under the duvet. I felt a light tap on my shoulder and I turned around to find him flashing his phone at me.

"It's okay to turn on the light if you need to. Use your phone. I don't mind." He retrieved his phone and added more messages. And flashed it back to me. "Please be comfortable with me. Do whatever you need to do." I easily acceded to Liam. At long last, I switched positions and unburdened my deadened side. I was on my back now like him. Both of us on our phones.

Messages started to emerge as soon as I connected my

phone—connected myself—to the rest of the world. The series of beeping sounds broke the calming silence of the night, but only for me.

"Please tell me where you are—Dad"

"Please tell me that you're safe and okay." This was another message from my father.

"Why did you turn off your phone again?" Message from Mom. And another one to call her back ASAP. I wondered if she knew that I had left Dad's place.

I willfully ignored them both and decided to message Liam instead. "Can't sleep like me?"

"Yes. Do you want to watch TV?" came Liam's quick reply.

"No. Not really. My eyes are tired but not my mind."

"Let's just talk then."

"So why can't you sleep?"

"I'm not used to sharing my bed."

I abruptly looked at him as soon as I read this. I was on my side now, facing him. "Sorry."

He also turned around to face me. "I'm not complaining."

"Have you ever been married?"

"No. But I was engaged once."

Blocked by the phones we were holding up close to our faces, we could only see one another's eyes—the lightest mocha darted straight to the darkest rocky road—our stares conjoint in the midst of silence and the soft glow from our phone screens. I wondered what sort of thoughts he was having as he looked at me intently. I suddenly imagined him as a lover, but I quickly broke away from this kind of contemplation.

I took my eyes back to the screen and wondered what possible things I could tell him—easy things. Before long, I got another message. He wrote, "Do you have kids?"

I was not ready to share stories about Willy so I chose my words carefully. "A son but he is not with me anymore."

"I'm sorry."

I didn't want to linger on this. "What's your favorite city among your travels?"

"Here. Manila."

"Really? I thought you hadn't seen anything yet except for the mall."

"The city I love, despite not having met her yet."

"How can that be?"

"Because it gave me this night."

I held my breath, then released it because I felt smothered.

"Have you been found?"

I was confused. "What do you mean?"

"Like your dad. Does he know where you are tonight?"

"Ah." Not a single soul. "No one knows where I am. You can sell my kidney and nobody will know."

"Ha-ha . . . I would, if I needed the money." Then he added, "Let me just steal your heart for myself."

"It's broken. Not much use in stealing it."

"You think? It might be worth a try."

"Do you really like me? Why?"

"I don't know. I just feel it."

Somehow deep in me, I knew what he meant. I was feeling that too.

He wrote, "What about you? Do you like me?"

"Why?"

"Why do I ask?"

"Why do you want me to say it when it feels like you already know?"

He gently took my hand to put my phone down. Nothing was between us now. I felt exposed so I lifted my phone again to hide my red face. I then sent, "You can't kiss me."

"Why not?"

"Because it's not right."

We were both quiet for a while. The night ended soon after. That's how we finished our first night. The next morning, his strapping arm was wrapped around my side while I was scooped restfully to his chest. It must have been somewhere between talks of what-ifs and why-nots that my mind finally gave up and slipped into slumber. Sleep was my excuse to break from the senseless talks that may have been too presumptive coming from the current muddle I was in. But I was not totally surprised that my subconscious went to his arms, the way I found myself when I woke up. I swiftly moved away to untangle myself from Liam, as much as a part of me wanted to stay.

CHAPTER 11

When the Rain Stopped Coming

"Have you ever been so lonely
that you speak
just to remind yourself
you have a voice?"
—Brian Galetto

California experienced a severe drought in 2014 that it had not felt for over fifty years. There was no anticipated substantial rainfall that could end this soon. It meant adapting to conservation measures being implemented by the state. Yes, these are the two things one cannot fight against or win over—death and Mother Nature.

Our apartment had a wooden planter box in the tiny backyard.

Kyle, a real handyman who loved to fix things, had built it originally as a sandbox for two-year-old Willy. When Willy grew bigger and lost interest in it, we converted it to try our hand at gardening.

"So, what do you want us to plant here?" Kyle asked Willy, only three at that time.

"Chaklate?"

"Chocolate? No, love. Just plants. You know, the green ones."

"Beanie stak?"

"Oh, like the one from Jack and the Beanstalk? Are you not scared of the giant?"

He shook his head proudly.

There was no reason for Willy to be scared. He always felt loved and protected. Except when he got sick. Then, we were useless parents. We failed our son.

I had been at the hospital far too long and had forgotten about our little garden. Willy, when he was still stronger, was in charge of watering the plants. He was eagerly looking forward to this harvest of pale red cherry tomatoes.

"He didn't even make it back home to see this." I said this with a heavy grudge while I discarded the tomatoes. I didn't want to taste any of them.

My mom came over the next morning. She brought me bagels and *pandesal*. She was looking through my fridge, perhaps making a mental note on what to bring me next. I had been seated at the same dining chair for hours now. "Do you know what's worse than hurting? It's not being able to feel anything at all." Before I could continue my wallowing, her arms were strapped around me, kissing the top of my head. Her sniffles grew and were as bad as mine.

• • •

I was glad for Kyle's anger. It kept a fire burning in the house. His frustrated shouts broke the uneasy silence all around us. It made it seem like there was some life left in the house, no matter how frail. I was beyond dead. Kyle once said, "I had two close calls with death—I have always wondered over how lucky I was to still be alive. I don't know why our son was never given this good fortune." We had no answer to this. Not one that was acceptable, justifiable, or helpful. We went on and on with this gut-wrenching question. This demand. "Why does it have to be our son?"

• • •

One afternoon after I had just gotten back from the grocery, I thoughtfully made dinner for Kyle and myself. Our meals had always been modified based on Willy's preferences. Baked macaroni and cheese was always out of a box and with powdered cheddar. I decided it was time to use sharper flavors like freshly grated Parmesan, Asiago, Havarti, and Gruyere, and substituted the elbow pasta with *tubetti rigati*. I was generous in using pepper and paprika, and sour cream with the milk. I sprinkled Italian seasoning and a drop of truffle oil. I laid breadcrumbs on the top layer. I finished it off with bacon bits before setting it in the oven.

"Do you like it?"

Kyle nodded hesitantly. In the past, he was the type who was very generous with his words. He was never reluctant to compliment my hair, the smell of the house, or the taste of a dish. Kyle and I loved how my revised recipe turned out, except for those unspoken words we both didn't have the heart to express—we had been much happier eating childlike meals with Willy next to us at the table.

. . .

In most of her visits, Mom never failed to advocate how I needed to find an activity for myself. It was less of a suggestion, more of a demand. "It will be healthy for your mind and spirit. Go back to work. Or go back to school. Whatever is easier. Just get out of the house." I started to work again as soon as I managed to keep my eyes dry. In a way, it would stop my worried mom from begging me.

Doris was the owner of the bakeshop I used to work at. She was also a friend. I didn't realize how I had missed Doris until she gathered me up against her and squeezed me for a tight hug when I stopped by for a visit. This gesture enabled me to respond earnestly and ask Doris for my job back.

The bakeshop had undergone some changes, but it was pretty much the same place as before. The walls were still painted bright egg-yellow, which seemed relevant for a bakeshop. It still served sandwiches and to-go bites. It still offered a crazy variety of muffins and artsy customized cakes. Being that it was located in the thick of the residential side of the Ventura harbor, it still had its regular crowd.

Since she already had a full-time storekeeper and baker, she took me in as her back-up manager. Without proper culinary education on my part, Doris took me under her wing as she patiently taught me the rudiments of baking and the business operations of a bakeshop.

Doris had been a great friend despite our age difference. Her age was closer to my mom's, but I saw her more as a friend. I confided in her often. She listened to my heartaches without the lectures, which my mom had a bad habit of dispensing, sometimes at the worst of times.

My initial attempts in baking fell flat. Literally. The cake did not rise.

"Remember, all ingredients should be room temp," Doris alerted me. "You have to set aside time for the chilled items to thaw out. The temp for wet items should be similar to the dry ones. And mix them slowly, alternate between the wet and dry, not all at once. But of course, avoid overmixing. Once it is in the oven, leave it alone so it bakes evenly. And when out of the oven, place on a cooling rack. Let it cool completely."

When I appeared overwhelmed, Doris added, "It's not hard. Okay, just two things. First, there's always a right time for everything, and second, don't worry if you missed the perfect time, because the world doesn't end there."

"Are we still talking about baking here?" I countered in my good-humored tone.

"Girl, of course we are," Doris validated, her tone easygoing. But then, in a more hesitant manner, she offered this, "I won't even try to stick my nose in your personal life. Or pretend to understand your journey, since I have never walked your path. I was never blessed to become a mother." Her voice now harbored a hint of sadness.

"Thanks again for taking a chance on me."

"Are you kidding me?" Doris tried to sound chirpy again. "I finally have a chance to enjoy retirement."

"Oh, please, Doris. You've been saying that even back when I was still single. The most you'll endure is semi-retirement. After that, you'll want to go back to the oven."

"Well, regardless . . . you only have a month to learn all my tricks. After that, it's all you. Better clear the mind of things beyond your control. Take things one day at a time. I meant the cake, one layer at a time."

All I managed to do was hug Doris tightly. She knew everything that had happened to me over the years. She was there at my wedding. And the baby shower. She had sent me spinach muffins for good lactation. She checked up on Kyle when he was in rehab for his legs. She had dropped off healthy organic cookies and cake pops for Willy a few times at the hospital. She had baked all of Willy's birthday cakes. She was there for me throughout, including during the funeral, the only time she didn't feel like baking. Even without saying much, Doris mourned with me. Willy was like a nephew to her.

She had Frank, the full-time baker, so my work seemed like playing in the kitchen decorating cakes. "The working hours of a baker will not help your marriage," Doris decided. It was a nice surprise to discover that I had a knack for baking and pastry arts. The last thing I wanted was to be a liability for Doris. As it turned out, I had enough passion in me.

There was a certain kind of elation whenever I poured flour in a mixing bowl and added the chilled butter that I had just cubed into smaller pieces. Together, I rubbed them with my fingertips as the coldness and moisture of the butter eased up to the dryness and the grains of the flour. With my thumb against my other four fingers, I kept rubbing the two ingredients in a steady stroke until they were no longer just flour and butter. Until I made crumbs out of the two. And both were no longer stuck being just what they used to be.

The tasks were basic, yet somehow they were therapeutic. There was an end goal to achieve. And somehow this was healing me. Simple things, like when I cracked some eggs and whipped them until the yolk became cotton-like. Then, when I scooped cups of sugar and whisked the white granules into the blend, I reveled with how the mixture disappeared into lovely white foam. Then when I added the vanilla extract until the froth seeped with fragrance, I relished the whiff of sweetness in my mind. I slowly poured in the flour and the baking soda, and watched how these dry ingredients were absorbed, losing their powdered element. When I added the milk, I gaped at how it clinched everything into a creamy fold. I felt the motion in my hands. I could taste my creation. It was not imagined. Not some happy but unattainable thoughts lingering in my head. It was in front of me.

When I fused edible pigments to create a new color, I marveled at how the right brightness of pink represented innocence and romance, or how the perfect tint of baby blue sky and sapphire sea embodied fun and adventure. And how the tinge of emerald, olive, and mint spoke of life and nature.

I was a completely different person whenever I was at the bakeshop, at the kitchen with the piles of baked and sweet treats and piping bags. I was excited to meet clients and work with them on whimsical designs and playful alternatives. It was more than a job. The bakeshop was an escape from the turmoil at home. I treated the bakeshop as if it was my own business. I worked long hours whenever required. I stayed out as much as I could.

"Are you home soon? Should I make salad for us? Or do you want me to grab a takeout somewhere?" Whenever I got this kind of call from Kyle, guilt sent me rushing home.

But as soon as I was home, seeing Kyle before me, I was Willy's mom again.

. . .

Kyle and I decided to give up the apartment we had rented for five years. There were just too many sad triggers for us. One morning he asked if I was feeling well enough for an errand.

"Kate, please have an open mind. I just want something for us. I realize there's nothing in this world that can ever replace our son, or make it better. But I want to do this for us. Don't give up on me, Kate. I'm not giving up on you."

Kyle took me house hunting.

He was right. There was nothing in this world that could make things better. But I had to stay afloat for him, or appear to, at least. The realtor moved at full throttle, and soon enough we had moved out of our two-bedroom apartment and into a three-bedroom townhome. I would have preferred a smaller property with fewer bedrooms, but most on the market had a minimum of three. When the realtor had said, "It will not be a huge difference in your monthly mortgage. Don't you want four bedrooms, in case you decide to have kids?" Kyle had to squeeze my hand, worried I might flare up. "We're only interested in three bedrooms," Kyle said firmly. The realtor never said a word about children again.

. . .

House moving was not a great idea after all. Going through Willy's bedroom was like walking into a landmine. Fragments of explosive emotions were uncovered with the scent of our son pervading almost everything I touched, his fresh-powder scent still lingering in the air, in my head. His presence was all over the room. The simple task of emptying Willy's closet, or putting his favorite books away, demolished all my strength and I fell in despair. I broke down. Once again.

"Do you want to donate some of his things?" Kyle saw me in a corner, weeping as I snuggled our son's baby blanket.

"How could you ask me that?"

"We can't live every single day like this, Kate!" Kyle pleaded.

"You forced this on me. I don't want a stupid house. I don't want to go through his things. I don't want to move. I don't . . . want . . ." I finally snapped. In my head, I heard myself say, *I don't want to live anymore.*

Kyle sat next to me. We were both on the floor for hours. Neither one had the energy to move along with our day.

• • •

I tried to survive for Kyle. Every morning, I pushed myself forward as I repeatedly told myself, "Try. To. Survive. For. Kyle."

We got the key to our new home three weeks before Thanksgiving. We immersed our grief in those big tubs of bluish gray, sage, and faded rose. We spent all our idle time painting the walls. We argued over what color for which room. It was a welcome distraction. It took our minds out of our misery. For a short while.

If there was a way to fast-forward or skip Thanksgiving, Christmas, and New Year's, Kyle and I would have done so without thinking twice. Friends and family insisted on coming over, or inviting us over. Kyle and I were on the same page on this—we were not ready to be around other people, even more so around our families. "Please, Mom. We'll join next time."

• • •

When you have been begrudgingly doing things long enough against your will, how do you keep showing up to life? When nights are even tougher than the mornings, where can you escape to?

Our drinking had been manageable. It became more frequent as miserable nights seemed to roll in more often than disappear. Getting drunk was our attempt at surrender, something we couldn't easily express when sober. After two or three glasses, when our nerves were calmer and alcohol overtook us, we were more forgiving about our sad fate. We were easier on ourselves. We were more human. Laughing seemed natural, not restrained. No guilt or remorse. We allowed ourselves to have fun. To feel normal. We even made passionate love.

I was seated by the kitchen counter. The cold touch of the granite stone was a stark contrast to the warm black French Roast coffee. It was a morning like the rest, except that I was sensing a throbbing headache while slowly remembering an impassioned night of two bottles of full-bodied dark ruby Bordeaux. I blankly stared at the tossed cushion pillows left on the wooden floor, which Kyle threw off to make space on the couch as he laid me down naked. As soon as he walked in to kiss the back of my head and drew the blinds up to let the morning light in, I guardedly asked him if he was trying to get me pregnant.

Without much thought, Kyle replied, "What's so bad about having another child?"

"You can't do that to me. You don't decide for us. We both have to want it."

"Oh, is that why you decided on your own to start taking birth control pills again? Really? I can't decide for us but you can?"

"It's not something new. I used to take them."

"But you stopped when we were trying."

"Exactly. When we were trying to have a child, which we are not doing now."

"When then?"

"When we're both ready."

"I'm ready."

"You're not ready, Kyle."

"I miss being a dad."

"That's the difference between us—I miss being a mom to *Willy*. Not just to anyone."

"That's not fair. I don't have to explain to anyone, including you, how I miss Willy!"

"Then, stop touching me just to get me pregnant!"

"I touch you because you're my wife. Because I miss you. I love you. And I want to feel loved!"

"Don't make it seem like I'm the bad guy here."

"Neither of one of us is the bad guy. We're on the same team here, Kate. Why do you keep pushing me away?"

"I'm not!"

"How come I feel alone then?" Kyle paused. He was probably as surprised as I was when he let out those words. But then, there was no sense denying it. He finished his point. "For a long time now." I had never seen Kyle as crestfallen as he was at that moment. I had nothing in me to make him feel better. I was in the same bad spot.

"I'm sorry if I can't attend to your feelings yet. I just buried a child."

"Kate, it also happened to me. He's my son too."

"Then prove it. Don't make me feel bad for not wanting to let go of Willy. Join me in my misery. Don't act like I'm asking too much when I need more time to grieve."

Kyle was silent. He looked resigned, or perhaps he was restraining himself from pushing this conversation any further. I realized too that it was pointless. Neither of us would win in this exchange of harsh words. It felt like we were a lost cause. He waited long enough to see if I was done talking. Then he picked up his car keys and drove away.

The last time Kyle and I had argued was during the initial stage of Willy's rigorous treatments. Understandably, we were all stressed, if not tired. That night after we fought, while the three of us lay in bed, Willy took my hand and Kyle's to put them together. Since then, I had avoided any kind of confrontation with Kyle for our son's sake. With Willy gone, even when it had been like walking on eggshells, I was amazed Kyle and I managed to walk out of every heated discussion before each one got worse.

I continued to take the birth control pills, and Kyle continued to ignore me. We sometimes gave in to our yearnings, but only when we were hammered, or simply too sad.

· · ·

It was Mother's Day weekend. Kyle and I were seated at the dining table, mindful of our phones. Conversations between us had been sporadic—perhaps our effort at keeping things simple, at a bare minimum. In his attempt to be thoughtful, Kyle asked if I wanted to go shopping, or get a spa. I was quiet so he went on with another plan.

"We can go to Universal Studios and have dinner at the Citywalk."

I practically choked on his pathetic idea.

"I promised Disneyland to Willy . . . ," I started calmly, but my anger grew too quickly, and I had no one to direct it at but Kyle. "He died not having set foot in a single theme park. What kind of childhood was that? What kind of parents are we? And to go now? Now that we don't have a child?"

I stormed out of the room. This must have frustrated him again, because I heard him kick the door.

Often, I tried not to express my thoughts because doing so would only hurt us both. Sometimes to be kind meant leaving words unsaid. But there were days like this when my wrath exploded into words.

Soon after, Kyle left a bouquet of red roses neatly arranged in a glass vase at the center of the kitchen counter. A notecard read,

> *My dearest Kate—I will always be grateful for having you as the mother of my child. Even with all the pain, I wouldn't change a thing in my life, except perhaps trade my life for his, if there was ever a chance, if it meant keeping Willy alive. It would make for a lesser tragedy. I don't know if there will ever come a time when we finally accept our son's fate. For now, I only ask that we don't give up on us. You'll always be a mom worth celebrating.*
>
> *Love,*
> *Kyle*

· · ·

September 2015. Kyle left for deployment. We both knew that the separation would be better for us. It had been fourteen months since our son's passing, yet we still didn't know how to be happy again, together.

"Give it time. I've seen you with Kyle during happier times. It's worth fighting for, right?" Doris reassured me.

The goodbye was not as bad as the last one. This physical distance was nothing compared to the emotional distance we'd had, which I supposed we had thought would get better if we kept on ignoring it.

• • •

One weekend, I drove myself to Disneyland. I spent my entire day riding on small boats and teacups. While on a caterpillar plane, I closed my eyes and imagined Willy holding on to me. Somehow, it freed me a little from my guilt. During our time apart, I did things that I wouldn't have done if Kyle was around. Often, I picked up fries and nuggets from his favorite fast-food places and munched them in my car while listening to Willy's favorite nursery songs. I kept this a secret because I didn't want my family and friends to think I had totally lost it.

I also took night classes and short courses. I took care of myself, of the things I needed to do while Kyle was away.

I went to my parents' house every Sunday. Halfway through one of our weekly dinners, my stepdad said to me, "It is good to be lost in the right direction."

"That's a good thing, right? Are you saying that I seem different these days?" I was happy to receive what I perceived to be a compliment.

"Kate, I see the progress too." My mom was quick to agree.

I nodded my head. I was not planning to argue with their premises.

Then, during one of his phone calls, Kyle said something similar to what my stepdad had implied the other night. "You sound like your old self."

"How? What do you mean?"

"You've been nagging me this whole phone call." We both laughed. We had not been like this for a while. It felt good to think we were really headed back to our old selves, to the right direction.

• • •

May 2016. Kyle came back after eight months of deployment. Our pain was still recognizable but so was our resolve to turn things around for us. It was a happy reunion. We missed each other greatly. It was evident the first few nights and mornings. We were like our old selves, like when we were newly married. We didn't need to be drunk or feel too lonely to crave one another's touch. It just came naturally, without inhibitions. We became sociable again.

"We missed you guys. We're so happy to see that you finally stopped avoiding our invites." That's what our friends repeatedly said to us during weekend BBQs and birthday parties. Kyle and I simply shrugged. We did not offer any explanations. They understood us.

• • •

One night, as we were in bed and Kyle was on top of me, he whispered, "Are you still on your pills?" When I said no, he said, "Fuck this, then" as he removed his rubber. On impulse, I pushed him off me.

"Why would you do that?" I asked angrily.

Kyle shook his head and said, "Never mind." He put his boxers back on and left the bedroom.

Kyle and I avoided each other for two weeks after that night. I stayed late again at work while he kept himself in the living room, drinking alone, watching TV, and deliberately passing out on the couch a few times.

He called me one afternoon while I was still at the bakeshop. "Are you staying late again?"

"Why? Do you want me to get dinner?" I was ready to make amends.

"We need to talk about my next billet."

"Okay, I'm leaving the bakeshop now. Do you want a burrito for dinner?"

Once home, while I was unwrapping the burritos and putting them on the plates, I noticed how uneasy Kyle seemed as he sat waiting for me to join him at the dining table.

"So, what did you want to talk about?" I asked as soon as I set the plate in front of Kyle. I tried to keep my voice as calm as possible.

"My detailer offered to move me to Gulfport, Mississippi. I want to take it, Kate."

"But that will be too far from Mom." The panic in my voice was apparent. "And what about the bakeshop?" There were so many things I would have to worry about if we left Oxnard.

"I think it's better for us to part ways, Kate. We should get a divorce." Kyle said this peacefully, with no hint of resentment or anger in his voice.

It was as if I was looking away, not minding where I was going, and I unexpectedly crashed hard against a wall. His words hit me with that kind of force. But I stayed quiet. I was out of words. I had no energy to fight it.

CHAPTER 12

When You Find
a Waterfall

*"The leaves through which the glad winds blew. Shared
the wild dance the waters knew; And where the shadows
deepest fell. The wood thrush rang his silver bell."*
—John Greenleaf Whittier

This could very well have been like many of those time-less stories. The moments I had with Liam were like the retelling of a multitude of fables and tales, all of them with happy endings, with Liam perfectly tailored to be prince charming. Except that I was not a maiden princess. And I couldn't assume a happily-ever-after end to this.

"They even have a waterfall." Liam had been trying to convince me to leave the city for a holistic escape encompassing mind, body, and spirit. And reality.

I, on the other hand, was the type that never put too much premium on cleansing and detox, or on meditative healing or a wellness spa—all the selling points of this getaway. "Will it be cheaper than this hotel?"

"Just come with me. The only favor I will ever ask of you."

My mom used to say to me, "Never say never. Or ever." My turn to hand it out like a life hack. "Fine. But we have to go to the mall so I can get some suitable clothes."

"It will be a private villa with its own pool. You won't need to bother with swimwear."

"I'm not swimming naked."

"Pajamas are acceptable. That was all I meant."

Liam knew when to back off whenever I called him out for being too daring. Of course, there was the chance that perhaps I was being too presumptuous.

We left the hotel and walked our way to the nearby mall. As soon as we arrived, I jiggled my hand from his clasp to alert him that we should stop. Then I grabbed my phone to text him.

"Let's separate and assign a meeting place for in an hour or so."

His instant reply was "Why?"

"I need to buy underwear."

"Okay." He smirked at me then went back to texting. "I'm just worried you won't find your way around. It's seriously a whole town, this mall."

"Yeah, I have the same thought. But I feel bad dragging you around to get my stuff. It's better to do our shopping separately."

"I have enough boxers. And I'm not swimming in Speedos, so I don't need to shop."

All I could do was laugh.

After three stores, two paper bags, and one hour of shopping, I texted him that I got everything I needed. Liam replied, "We have enough time for lunch before we check out of the hotel and head to the resort. It's your turn to decide on where to eat."

"Sushi?"

"Sure, let's find a place."

I had not been to a sushi place for years now, after I married Kyle. Liam seemed to be open to any cuisine.

"You don't seem picky with food."

"No, I'm not."

Before I could compliment him for this, I received another text. "Just picky with women." I knew he was watching my reaction so I gave it to him. An eye-rolling retort to complement my flushed cheeks.

· · ·

We were headed to a town named after Santa Rita, the patron saint of lonely hearts. A billboard to welcome travelers read, "Sweet Saint Rita, patron of loss and loneliness. Please help me find a friend to lead me out of this dark place." I snickered at the relevance to us.

We arrived at the holistic retreat after two hours of alternating between crawling traffic and bouncy speed as we traversed from the densely inhabited city to laid-back smaller towns and rural spaces. Our final destination was unerringly truthful to the term sanctuary—it was apparent that nature was highly venerated. Birds had first names, leaves were eaten, and rocks had healing power. Thankfully, everyone was wearing typical clothing, so I didn't freak out.

As we were being led to our assigned chambers, we passed by traditional stilt houses made of bamboo and coconut husks, which looked way swankier than those indigenous huts I saw when I was growing up. We were walking on golf-course-quality lawn, plush and evenly manicured, with patches of pearly white pebbles to accentuate the verdant setting. I could only recall stepping on muddy soil or burning hot, cracked ground when I was younger. We must have been really poor.

We were almost at the dead end, on the alpine side of the resort, when the guide steered us to our modern villa. It was situated on the pressed-flat part of the hill, a cul-de-sac of four units. Each one was camouflaged against shrubs and forest enclosure. We were assigned a stone cottage with a rustic mahogany double door—the only part visible in the frontage as the rest of the structure appeared to be tucked in a jungle. Greeting us at the entrance was an opulent poster bed with net drapes on each post. It was reminiscent of my dad's mosquito net, but that had seemed like a purchase from a thrift store while this was obviously handmade. The glass accordion door led to an open-space balcony, which doubled as a dining area but also included a lounging corner consisting of a daybed for lovers to sprawl on while gazing at the sky.

From the balcony, a wooden staircase took us down to a breathtaking outdoor infinity pool. It was narrow, about the size of four rectangular bathtubs combined, but the forest backdrop was hard to ignore. It was simply stunning. Right below the bedroom and adjacent to this intimately cozy pool was a bathroom suite. Well, not just a suite, more like a haven of its own. As we walked in to inspect the bathroom, I could see the gleaming waterfall showerhead enclosed in glass was on full display. Whoever would be showering would be on full display too.

Liam and I looked at each other—I imagined he was also

wondering if this ultra-modern bathroom allowed for any privacy. I relaxed as soon as I saw a changing space and a separate water closet with frosted-glass sliding doors, across from two large farm-house vintage vanity sinks. In the corner, where the roof ended, was a spa tub bolstered in an open space next to a stand of young bamboo trees.

I had an impulse to lightly punch Liam in his toned bicep. He replied with a wink. Because he never spoke a word to me, whenever he needed to prod me to move along, Liam would simply take my hand to lead me away. Except this time, there was only me and him, alone in this intimate setting, among the quiet and the trees. In this discreet lair within the wilderness. When he took my hand as we ascended back to the bedroom, and as we lay down on our backs and rested our thoughts, I had already begun to wonder how I would manage to separate passion from reason.

Liam led me to our appointed body scrub and mud treatment. I was given the option to wear skimpy sheer thong underwear and a small towel to cover up after I came out of the changing room. Besides, I was wearing nothing else under my dress, as I was using my limited undergarments sparingly. Liam, in his glorious chiseled form, was already lounging facedown on the massage table with a small towel strategically covering his bum. For a second, I felt like volunteering to massage him myself. I had to whisper to the masseuse that the guy I was with had never seen me naked, so it would be her job to cover me up in order to keep it that way. But I worried for nothing. Our minds and bodies needed this massage badly. Liam and I fell asleep almost instantly, even while our bodies were being caked in mud.

I was starting to wake up as I felt the warm, spongy cloth being rubbed on my skin. After the mixture was removed and our bodies cleansed, we headed to dinner. It was grilled mushroom, eggplant, and zucchini salad for him while it was arugula and jicama mix for me. We enjoyed the healthy dishes, but we also relished the thought that, back in the room, Liam had a bag stuffed with all the junk food and red wine we had managed to sneak in. When he swiped his hand from his lips to his cheeks, I naturally responded by wiping my face of any stains or food particles. He smiled, so I figured whatever was on my face was gone. Little did I know that it was a sign for kiss, until he told me after dinner.

As I got to know him more, it was hard to ignore how attractive he was. He was tall and sexy. Not burly sexy, more like athletic sexy. He was in between handsomely rough and sensibly easygoing.

"Oh my gosh," I excitedly texted Liam. "I figured out who you remind me of." Since the day we met, I had been racking my brain trying to make out who Liam bore a resemblance to. It was only now, when I was comfortable looking at him closely, that I finally saw more of him.

Liam looked at me with wide-open eyes as if to say, I'm waiting, let's hear it.

"Paul Rudd." I was intently watching how Liam would react to this.

I was so surprised to finally hear him talk. "You mean, I don't strike you as Captain America or Thor? I'm Ant-Man to you." That Paul Rudd remark elicited such a strong contention on his part that he suddenly blurted out his sentiments into words. Into sounds. Into a voice. His voice. Low and breathy and husky. Sexy voice. From a delicious mouth.

"Hey," I protested, typing as quickly as I could, while trying to explain my opinion. "You make it sound like it was such a bad thing. Paul Rudd is adorably sweet. His eyes are so genuinely charming. Just like yours." I omitted the part that my brain was telling me to add—soft, kind, and lustful.

Liam smiled and said, "Well, as long as you have the hots for Ant-Man among The Avengers, then I'll take it." Liam said it a little loud, and I almost wanted to hide under the table as soon as I caught a guy listening to our conversation.

As I recovered from that comment, I texted, "I don't compare men. Do you?"

"I don't compare men either." Even louder than the Avengers comment.

I gave him a glare. Hopefully not a frightening or mean kind, just the soft stop-it sort. "Seriously, that's one thing we should never talk about—our exes. If you must know, I'm unreasonable when I'm jealous."

He texted back, "Oh, believe me. I have the hots for jealous and unreasonable."

I laughed so hard at how embarrassingly funny his comments had been, and how he purposely made it loud for everyone in the room to hear. It was clear he didn't care what anyone else thought.

Liam followed it up with a text. "Sorry if it was over-the-top loud. It was fun. Liberating."

And to that I leaned across the table to plant a kiss on his lips. It was soft and quick, but it shook me nevertheless.

He wrote, "When can I do that to you?"

All I could do was shrug my shoulders.

Liam shrugged back and typed his response: "Okay, let's make a deal. Talk of past relationships is the only thing off the table."

We strolled slowly back to our villa. My strappy, short white swing dress left me bare against the cool sundown breeze. Everything around me felt perfect. This refuge was true to its name. I was more lenient to myself. Some soft flickering stars added sparkle to the evening. It seemed like they were within reach. Lively sounds of crickets broke the tranquility and silence. It also felt like the noise outside was irrelevant to the serenity within. And that I had a hand to hold, to reassure me that I don't have to be alone.

Liam must have known, by the way I chomped on my dish, that I needed sugar and salt. He invited me to the balcony where we shared a bottle of Australian Shiraz, a bag of BBQ chips, and a bar of sea salt caramel dark chocolate. From the corner of my eye, I knew he was watching me. I had been dodging his glances.

He moved his chair straight to my line of sight. With the back of his palm supporting his chin, he was slightly leaned forward so our eyes could meet. When he had my attention, he straightened up. He wiped his forehead across, left to right, then placed his right hand over his right shoulder, the palm facing his body. Perhaps he meant to signal that I should wipe the burden off my shoulder, or that he would.

"Forget the past, Kate," Liam said in a faint tone, almost a whisper.

I looked away, forcefully and to the side, to tell him I had purposely been eluding him so he should stop chasing my gaze.

He stood up and outstretched an arm, his open palm in front of me. It was an invitation to take his hand. To somewhere. Or something. To not accept was futile at this point. I was already into him, well before I took his hand.

Hence, I took it. Thoughtlessly. No, it was in fact the opposite. It was after much pondering. After I had decided to allow myself to feel something other than pain again. I'm human. A woman. About to get divorced. I had cried more than my fair share. I knew that I should free myself from this unhappiness. I wanted this for myself.

I wanted Liam.

He took me downstairs and we stepped into the quiet blue water, fully clothed. It was warm enough that the only shivers I felt were all drawn from Liam. I was following his lead, his hand gripping mine, as we moved deeper into the pool. He was still in his shirt and shorts while I was in my white dress. He placed me in a corner where I stood unmoving, waiting. Water right below my chest. He descended into the water, his hands holding the side of my hips. As he gradually moved up, his hands also advanced upward. From the hips, his squeeze turned into a gentle stroke to the sides of my breasts. He then emerged from the water, catching his breath until he caught mine. The thought of his mouth on my mouth had lingered in my head for so long. It was happening now, making me shudder and ache for more. Until he breathed on me something I had long gasped for—resurgence of life.

Liam kissed me with lustful desire. It was lifting. I needed him as much as he needed me. They were slow, deepening kisses, gradual and lasting and unhurried. They hinted that this was not in passing or a one-night affair. Like we knew we had time, as much time as we had spent waiting for exactly this kind of moment.

He sucked on my lips for a longer second until he let go, his face at a thread-like distance from mine. He leaned his forehead against mine. I closed my eyes, like I was supposed to receive his thoughts.

We both heaved a deep sigh. I motioned to lift his shirt. As soon as he removed it, heavy with water so that it fell away with a thud, I kissed his shoulders. I had been wanting to taste this. Him. He parted my hair and ran his tongue on the side of my nape.

He gently slid the straps off my shoulders. My dress, however, still floated on its own so he plunged himself downward into the water again as he pulled my dress off me. I had nothing else on underneath. He emerged with my dripping dress and tossed it next to his shirt.

Liam carried me sideways, my quivering body draped in his arms. My clasp flung to his neck. He laid me on the first step of the pool. My upper body halfway rested between the ground and the pool. My hips sprawled on the top part of the pool unsubmerged. He knelt on the lower steps, facing my exposed form, tasting me. Relishing the woman between my legs. Savoring the aroused spot that was about to sanction his vigor. I imploded. I propped up and lifted his face to show I was quenched, that I wanted him inside me. And so, he made his way. He thrusted into my realm. Tenderly. He pounced deeper. With more speed. Toward his high point. In this witching hour of the night. And as he released himself, he let out a groan. A short hissed followed by my name.

CHAPTER 13

When You're Overdue for Happiness

"I measure every grief I meet
with narrow, probing eyes—
I wonder if it weighs like mine—
or has an easier size."
—Emily Dickinson

On the fourth day, the sun, moon, stars, and all the bright planets were created. God gave us all these luminaries to provide us with rays of light. How could one possibly leave a beautiful night without worries of not being able to see the same marvel when the sun comes up? Whenever something good happened to me, I always had trouble sleeping. I never wanted a good day to end with the fear that after the good comes the bad days. How do you trust and let yourself be comforted by the idea that the sun and the moon give out equal brilliance?

It was a charming morning of faint breeze against mellow sun. I woke up to a soothing playlist of bamboo flute, Celtic harp, and wind chimes. Liam was playing some healing ambient music for me. Unless it was a pounding beat, he couldn't feel a single rhythm, so this was clearly for me. He was seated by the dining table, his hand with a pen as he intently drew diagrams on a paper. A breakfast feast was already set up and waiting for us. He was literally a dream boy.

When I swathed my arms around him and kissed the top of his head, he turned around to lock his lips on mine. I instantly stepped back and gestured an explanation why I was refusing his kiss by covering my mouth while pinching my nose. He laughed with some hint of a sound.

Breakfast was heavenly cut-up fruits in coconut bowls and *kapeng barako*. The whiff of roasted beans and sweet chocolate summoned me to hug the warm cup with both hands as I enjoyed the aroma before tasting the robustness of this native coffee grown right below the city.

After we cleared up the table, Liam and I played Build Your BINGO. He was busy organizing this game while I was being a sleeping beauty. He explained the rules. "First, be truthful. Second, fill out all the blank boxes with answers about impressions of each other. Each must have a key word that begins with B, I, N, G, O. Example: under the B column, if I were to answer this, I would say you're a baker."

Wow. Did I ever tell him that I work at a bakery?

"Your answers would be your perceptions of me, and mine would be of you. Once all fifteen boxes are filled out, we exchange papers. We checkmark all correct assumptions. Winner will decide penalty for the losing player."

And so, we began this interplay of getting-to-know-you game. Like test-driving or food sampling. Was this a compatibility test? Figuring out personalities and quirkiness could be a good or bad thing, both for the subject and responder. I guess this was a risk we were willing to take to really get to know each other. If not for anything else, just for fun.

After a long, contemplative evaluation of this unexpected gorgeous creature right next to me, I completed the BINGO card with these insights about Liam.

B for barefoot at home, banana breakfast kind of guy, baseball for sports, bearded during winter, hero-brave.

I for introspective planner, impractical shopper, instigator, instructor, independent.

N for nature-lover, naughty in bed, noncommittal, night-owl, nonconformist.

G for generous son, generous brother, generous friend, generous lover, great sex.

O for ocean-lover, lots of one-night stands, on the move always, on the fence with marriage, observant.

When we went over my answers, it turned out I had four mistakes.

His BINGO paper revealed these insights about me.

B for beautiful, easily bored, between shy and bold, between sad and very sad, broken heart.

I for inspiring, impulsive, irrational when upset, intriguing almost secretive, intense lover.

N for nurturing, novice to pain, numb inside, new traveler, nagger.

G for graceful, great body, giving, grateful, giggle laugh.

O for old-school-conservative, overwhelmed, obedient to rules, obligates self to a fault, overdue for happiness.

I cried after I read the list that Liam made about me and ran downstairs to the bathroom, but it was so huge it gave me no privacy. I was washing my face when Liam appeared, ready to console me.

"I'm sorry if I made you upset in any way," Liam said.

I shook my head. Put my hand on his chest then shook my head again. I hope he understood that it wasn't his fault. Except for novice to pain, he got everything right. Even some of the ugly truths about me. He knew my pain but he had no idea that the pain had hovered in me far too long. *Was I really overdue for happiness?*

Liam took me for a stroll. Halfway through our walk, under the swaying palm trees, along the layers of birds of paradise in orange and red, among watchful guests, and in the middle of the pathway, he kissed me gently. We were out in the open, showing true emotions. Liam raised a hand flat open facing me, and bent his little finger with his thumb, leaving the index, middle, and ring upright. Spread apart, the three digits formed the letter W. When I mouthed the letter to him, he nodded to give me affirmation. With both of his hands formed in W, sideways, right hand under left, he moved his right hand in a circular fashion to loop over and rested it on top of the left. I must have had a blank look on my face, so he went to whisper "world" in my ear then proceeded to brush his gentle lips from my ear to my cheeks, a soft peck as he moved away. Then, he raised his index and middle fingers to his eyes like it was meant to say watch, or see. He followed it by repeating the world sign. He motioned two fists to join each other then pointed his index at himself.

"See the world with me." He used his voice to make sure I understood clearly. I grinned at the thought of that phrase. I had no phone, or pen and paper to express my thoughts. I wished, in that moment, that I knew how to sign. Or had the right answer. And so, I took his hand so we could resume our stroll. The world would have to wait. And there was still that waterfall to see anyway. The sound of cascading water was soothing—if only Liam could hear it. There's a certain balance in hearing the trickles of water while watching the perpetual flow. It's like being in a bubble, except you are not trapped. There's still energy in motion.

We learned that a waterfall symbolized the descent of light and cognizance. Liam pointed to the water to ask if I wanted to go in. I waggled my head. Perhaps I was not ready to receive the flowing water and its sublime cleansing just yet.

When we realized there was a motorbike for hire, Liam hurriedly arranged for our trip to the town. I almost wanted to tell him that I would just swim with him in the waterfall instead, but it was a challenge to explain this part. Besides, I saw how excited he got looking at the map of the area. My BINGO card should have included "not a daredevil." I was never a risk taker, not in life and not in love. But perhaps there was a new me beginning to bud.

Liam swiped all my hair to the back, gently placed the helmet on me, and pressed the strap together. The click of the snap being secured startled me, perhaps because I was in a trance once I placed my starry eyes on his.

"We'll be fine," Liam said. "I won't let anything bad happen to you. Do you trust me?" I nodded as he placed his lips on mine. I waited for Liam to put his helmet on, and hopped on as soon as he was seated on the bike.

And it turned out, the bike ran more like a scooter.

I sat behind Liam—my clasp unbreakable. Almost clingy.

Liam and I headed to the wet market. Even from a distance, the sweet stench of the sea and the burning charcoal had already hailed us as we approached the first vendor. There was an option to buy fresh seafood and vegetables, which nearby kiosks would cook for a fee. When a white guy like Liam appeared in the market, all the local vendors cajoled him, waving their hands at him as if he was a VIP shopper. Liam held on to me tighter. It was now his turn to be a little afraid.

It was easy being with Liam. It was easy to laugh. It was easy to be happy. We walked around the market. Around town. Sat on the grass. We watched as people passed by. Watched them glance back at us. Girlfriends parading their smiles around town. Small kids running around in one big batch. A family of three. A couple.

"Wow, we didn't find one person walking alone," Liam said aloud.

"Nobody wants to be alone," I said softly, mainly to myself.

We then walked to an old-looking Catholic church, which was holding a wedding at that moment. We curiously stood by the door, observing this celebration of life, of love.

"*Libre pumasok sa simbahan.*" The candle vendor a short distance from us said this. She was announcing that entrance to the church was free, to nobody in particular. But it almost felt like it was directed to us, even though she was not looking in our direction. She was blind.

As we turned our backs and moved away from the church, the blind lady said again in a more mysterious voice, "*Ako'y bulag pero hindi kailangan ng mata para makakita.*" Translated, this meant, "I may be blind, but you don't always need eyes to see."

We strolled a little longer around town until it started to get dark, then we decided to head back to the resort. All the while, my head still lingered around those words spoken by the candle vendor.

When we returned to our room, I was pointing at myself and then at Liam, in an attempt to figure out who would shower first—he misunderstood and thought I suggested we shower together. I realized I would have to learn how to sign "or." When he took my hand and brought me downstairs, I was still waggling my head. He took me past the shower stall and into the end corner, where lighted candles were positioned on the ground, around the tub. As we got closer, I was surprised to see the immaculate white tub brimmed with warm coconut milk, Moroccan oil, and lavender-scented sea salt, as described on a cardstock label placed on the ledge. Next to a single-stem white lily.

"I supposed this would be something ladies dig. At least it's what the resort manager suggested. Give me a thumbs-up if I did good," Liam said proudly with a wink.

Instead of a thumbs-up, I clutched my hands together around his neck and pulled him into a hug. I rested my head on his chest—his heart, I reckoned, was within reach. I led him in a slow dance. There was no music to accompany our sway, just the soft rustling sound of the bamboo trees and the words I hummed in my head—"We've got tonight . . . who needs tomorrow."

After a short while, Liam kissed my forehead and reached for both of my hands to unclasp them from an embrace. "Save me another dance sometime. Right now, it's good to get into the tub while the coconut milk is warm. I'll grab myself a chair and drinks for both of us."

When he came back, I was already immersed into the creaminess of the oil and milk, and allayed by the luscious fragrance of the coconut and lavender. I tried to straighten my upper body without revealing my breasts and folded my legs to make room for Liam. He shook his head. "That's all yours. I prefer the coconut scent on you than on me. I'm happy to sit out here." He said this while handing me a glass of red wine.

"Is it really relaxing?"

I bobbed my head extensively—a simple nod would have diminished my account of how much I enjoyed this.

I raised my glass and gestured a toast. Liam obliged by lightly clicking his drink against mine. "Cheers to you, Kate. And to many more nights like this."

After a big sip, I placed my glass on the floor and motioned my free hand in the air to draw a question mark. He smirked and then said, "Go on. Hit me with your question." I then repeated by mouthing the word "why" while drawing the question mark in the air.

"Ah, okay . . . 'why,'" he said.

I excitedly nodded. I proceeded to point my finger at Liam, which he acknowledged by saying, "Me, or I."

I nodded again. I continued and patted my throat, then steered my index finger at my chest. Liam recounted my hand motions one by one. "Why . . . me . . . neck . . . you?"

It didn't make sense when Liam connected the words together. I shook my head and decided to point at my neck, then my mouth, and then motioned the tips of my fingers together as if it was a mouth talking.

I was never good at playing charades, unfortunately.

I repeated the whole ensemble. When it started to make sense to Liam, he articulated the question. "Why I talked to you? Or I guess, why I use my voice to you?"

I followed this with my index finger downward while mouthing the word "now," then motioned my thumb away while shaking my head as I spelled out "not before" in my mouth.

"I think I understand what you're trying to ask me," Liam slowly said.

Why use his voice now but not then?

"I've just gotten so used to signing. Sometimes I just forget to use my voice. Other times, maybe I prefer not to use it. I feel so disconnected with it. It doesn't help that I can't hear myself speak, so I avoid using my voice."

I gently nodded to acknowledge his explanation.

Once I saw Liam had finished his drink, I invited him to join me in the tub with the crude signals of my hand. "I don't think there's room for two," Liam said, to which I readily met his gaze with a puppy face.

With a faint outbreath, he warned me jokingly, "You asked for it. You better be ready for me." Liam took off his shirt and pants, leaving his boxers on. He went in behind me, with my body now squeezed in between his long legs. He gently pulled my back to his chest with his arms encircled around me.

Liam started to stroke my neck with his lips as he said teasingly, "My first time to taste coconut milk. I love it." Despite limited flexibility, and with my back to him, we persisted in fooling around in the tub.

When Liam whispered in my ear how he would give up all the practical things he got just to be able to hear what music we were dancing to, I swallowed a big lump of sadness. I decided to turn around and kneel before him. I caressed his face with both of my pruney hands and searched for his eyes. The blues were gone. He pursued my strokes by running his mouth along my skin, beginning from my arm and moving toward my breast, then to my neck, and ending with his lips pressing against mine in a hungering, lingering kiss.

When we couldn't bear it any longer, Liam took me upstairs, where we made love, this time in the comfort of the four-poster bed.

CHAPTER 14

When the Empty Song Repeats Itself

"I have spread my dreams under your feet;
Tread softly because you tread on my dreams."
—William Butler Yeats

O ne message from Kyle. "Let's talk. Please come home."

I woke up abruptly—I had been dreaming about my mom. It was nothing distressing or peculiar. For whatever reason, my conscious mind interrupted that dream and goaded me to get up. I left the bed and checked my phone. That was when reality finally pulled me back to earth. To the ground, below the cloud nine I had been on for a few days now. This was the downside to too much fun. If allowing myself to laugh again or permitting myself to feel great about my existence had caused the imbalance in my life, then I must be on a downward spiral again. Whenever I was on neutral, everything was at a balance. But I had since soared to seventh heaven, so of course I should have expected that there was nowhere to go but down. What goes up must come down.

It was early in the morning, shortly after the dawn broke. I sat on the daybed alone, a blanket wrapped around my shaking body. I could almost feel the low clouds and the fog with the cooler breeze that traversed through this open sundeck. My body felt the chills from the cooler temperature. And then from the short text message from Kyle.

The ripple it created ripped the serenity I had been relishing. I wondered what Kyle was thinking when he sent me this one message. Or what he would be thinking if he learned about Liam. That I had been with another man. And shared his bed. That another man had been inside me. And that he would always be inside my head, assuming I went back to California.

• • •

The sun was already seething in a ball of fire when I was startled by a ringing tone. It was my mom calling again. I must have gone back to sleep on the daybed while I mulled over my situation. I found Liam in bed reading a book. He didn't even look up at me.

I joined him in bed, unsure how to greet him. Or if I even needed to explain why I was sleeping on the balcony and not next to him. I sat on the bed, facing him and with my legs crisscrossed. I stared at him until he looked up to acknowledge me. I smiled, then proceeded to kiss him on the mouth. I greeted him with "good morning," making sure he could see my lips as they formed the words.

I held my phone out while mouthing the words, "We need to talk." Liam got up from the bed to grab his phone.

"Know that I'll understand. I'll fight for you but only if you let me," Liam said casually while at the balcony.

Without looking back to Liam, I went to my phone and entered a reply. "My husband sent a message for me to come back home." This was the kind of conversation I preferred not to do over a text, but what choice did I have? I waited for Liam to reply or come back to bed, but neither happened.

I then added, "I don't know what to do." Still no reply. I looked back to find Liam gone, his phone on the table. He was already downstairs, seated by the pool, gazing past its infinity edge.

I joined him, sitting down next to him at the edge of the pool. I handed him his phone so we could continue to talk. He took it from me and placed it on the side as he began to speak.

"I always keep my promise. I asked you for a few days so we could try to get to know each other, but I think it's time to go home. You probably want the same thing. You don't have to give me a reason, or give yourself grief. It's best that you go back to your husband anyway. Let's arrange our flights and depart tomorrow."

This rendered me speechless. Undercut. Deposed. He had just marshaled me back toward my old life without even asking what I wanted to do. As if he had finally become dog-tired of me. Like this was some escapade that seemed to bore him now. That I was some low-hanging fruit that was easy to pull into his adventure but I didn't measure up to his expectation. Without reservations, he was chucking me out of his life. He hadn't even given me any time to choose what I wanted to do. With us. I guess there really was none of that. There was no us.

I texted him, then went back to the room to start booking my flight. "Oh, don't worry about offending me or hurting my feelings. One thing you got wrong about me—I'm not new to pain. It didn't take long for you to get tired of me. Buyer's remorse is not uncommon. I think it's three days from the date of purchase. Don't bother explaining. I certainly was not given a chance to." Sent.

CHAPTER 15

When All the Cars Have Left

"If you can bear to hear the truth you've spoken."
—Rudyard Kipling

L iam took some time to read what Kate had to say. It was a series of back-and-forths in his mind. He was very close to taking his words back. He had that nagging feeling that what he just said to Kate was a mistake. But there was also a small part of him that pushed to cut off his ties with Kate. He felt it was the decent thing to do. And so, until he felt set and convinced that it was the right thing to do, to let Kate go, Liam didn't touch his phone. He let time pass, enough time for decorum to overcome his emotions. His head was clouded with the notion that what transpired between him and Kate was wrong. Until he persuaded himself, he couldn't let his feelings rule him.

Liam sat alone and waited for Kate to come back. Perhaps to tell him how it made sense to end what they had. Perhaps she wasn't ready to go through with her divorce. She didn't need to explain this to him. It made sense for them to start rebooking their flights soon. When Liam finally checked his phone to read what Kate had said, it broke his heart. The way he saw it, she had perceived that he had broken hers.

"Fuck. I am so stupid." Liam released his anger.

Liam hurriedly went back to the room upstairs, but Kate was not in sight. He grabbed his shoes and walked around the sanctuary. He scoured the entire resort but did not find her. His heart competed with his mind as he raced around looking for her. He had to have a chance to explain to her. He had to know what she wanted to do about them. He didn't handle this well at all. He felt like a moron. Fuck.

"Have you seen Kate? The woman I'm with." As soon as the receptionist started talking, he rudely interrupted her. "Write it, please! I'm Deaf!" Liam couldn't hear himself, but he was positive that his tone and expression had offended her. "I'm sorry. I'm just in a hurry," Liam said more softly, though it was hard to tell.

She wrote, "Sir, ma'am Kate left for the airport. Ninoy Aquino International Airport. I booked the car for her."

"Can you book me a car too? To the same airport."

She handed him another note to say that all their cars were out for the rest of the day. Liam couldn't help it and released a banging "fucking fuck" that must have startled every single person in the sluggish town.

CHAPTER 16

When You Count That Day

*"Tell no one else its contents, never its secrets
share; When you've dropped in your care and
worry, keep them forever there."*

—Bertha Adams Backus

Summer 2007

L iam and Julia always ended up with too many muffins, more than his own liking, but he was not going to admit this to Julia.

He had stopped by the bakeshop on his way home, with two ideas playing in his head. First was to get a cupcake. Second, he had hoped to see the girl who worked there up close and perhaps introduce himself to her. Only, she was not working at that time.

Probably a good thing—what was he thinking, anyway, introducing himself to girls when he was getting ready to propose. He then asked the bakeshop to put a heavier icing on the cupcake where he would hide the engagement ring.

When he got home and offered the tiny cake to Julia—insisting that she just try it—she wouldn't even touch it.

"Oh, you went to the bakeshop? I'm kinda full. Maybe later."

If only Julia had taken more interest in his surprise sweet treat, she would have seen the ring then. Liam, for the rest of the evening, watched Julia and the cupcake so she wouldn't choke on it or accidentally toss the ring away. She was about to go to bed when he asked her again if she was ready for her dessert. How many clues did the girl need? This just wasn't working out. "I can't have that right now!" Julia had decidedly said, before heading off to brush her teeth.

Liam shrugged his shoulders and said, "No worries. You probably didn't miss much." For the time being, he would stow the ring away for a later day.

• • •

"Has Julia been baking? These are good." Kyle had grabbed the banana caramel, his second treat after the carrot muffin he had just chomped through seconds ago.

Liam had been bringing the muffins every Monday morning to work. He snuck them out to bring to the office while Julia was out on her morning jog.

Liam chortled. "I wish." Either Julia was just trying to humor him whenever he suggested they pick up some treats at the bakery on Sundays, or she just liked smelling them and looking at them. She, however, would not eat them. Her body couldn't tolerate sugar and carbs. Clearly—not even when it meant hidden diamonds and buried treasure! No matter. Liam, on the other hand, enjoyed watching the young Asian woman more than he cared about the baked goods themselves, so he was happy to bring five of the six leftover muffins to work.

"Where do you get them?" Kyle wanted to know.

"It's too far to describe." Liam, in truth, preferred not to share where he had been getting his weekend treats. She was his secret indulgence. It was harmless. He was just curious about her.

"Are you all set with your transfer?" Kyle inquired. Liam and Kyle were work friends, and to some extent they even treated each other like brothers. They'd worked together for three years. Kyle was a considerate coworker and a well-meaning friend. He always kept the office laughing with his stories. It was fun to be around him. During lunch, Liam was at ease because he didn't have to eat and talk—a combination Liam didn't particularly enjoy. Kyle, on the other hand, was happy to talk most of the time while Liam stayed quiet. They often hung out on weekends. In fact, Kyle had dated Snow, Julia's friend, until Snow had to move to Seattle for a job. They'd dated for over a year but it had been so casual that Kyle had not even chewed on the idea of stopping her. On the flipside of the coin, Snow was more hopeful and had viewed the relationship more intensely. It was more of a litmus test, as Julia had explained to Kyle and Liam one evening, weeks after Snow had left.

"Kyle, you do know that Snow was just waiting for you to stop her?" Naturally, Julia could not help but give Kyle grief on his breakup from her friend.

Liam and Julia had gotten used to being around Kyle and Snow—two couples on weekend trips, Friday night dinners, and Sunday beach outings. Somehow it made Liam a little sad that the other pair had broken up, and he knew Julia felt the same way. Liam and Julia had been living together for years while Snow and Kyle had never shared an apartment. Liam was fully aware that Kyle knew it was a test, and that he had wanted to fail it.

"What can I say? We weren't ready. I wasn't ready," Kyle said in his defense, the smirk on his face too apparent.

"Ready for what?" Liam could see how Julia was too eager to help this other couple patch things up. She believed that they were good together. She missed Snow. She missed seeing them as a couple. He couldn't blame her.

"Dude." Kyle turned to Liam for help. "Tell her what I mean."

Liam pretended to laugh. He played the ignorant card, unqualified to explain to his girlfriend that Snow was, perhaps, simply a passing thing. Kyle was loyal to the relationship but was ready to move on as soon as it was over. As soon as Snow demanded more.

Things were different with him and Julia. They had been together for so long it felt almost like they were related. They had been around each other most of their lives, so much so that Liam didn't know any different. It was like when one was born into a family—that family was all you had, the only kind of love you knew, the kind you were used to. Julia was that to Liam, but also so much more. She was his first crush, first kiss. She was his prom queen. She went with him whenever the Navy had to relocate him. She was his secondary case of emergency, his secondary benefactor in case of death—secondary to Liam's mother. In more ways, she was more than a girlfriend. She was his best friend. Almost a wife.

They were moving back to Little Creek, Virginia, in three weeks. He had decided to invite some friends to a going-away dinner on their last Friday in Oxnard, five days before they moved out. He had been debating whether to put a ring on Julia. He thought he might surprise her with the long-overdue proposal.

"Kyle, dinner on Friday. Not this one but the next, at Conchita's. Bring a date," Liam said to his friend.

Kyle raised both palms up and rejected Liam's suggestion. "What date? And miss my chance of hooking up with one of Julia's friends?"

"You've been banned. You're not allowed anymore. Not from her list of friends. They're all friends of Snow too."

Kyle ignored the warning. "We shall see."

Conchita's Grill & Cantina was not as trendy as Julia had hoped for, but Liam had insisted on having their going-away dinner there. "It's authentic and fresh and unpretentious. Hard to get this in Little Creek." He was adamant. He knew that the predominantly bright orange-and-lime exterior made Julia wince. The mustard walls inside made it all worse for her à la mode taste. She had wanted a chic brewery or a classic sit-down Italian for their going-away dinner. But it only took a little convincing to sway her to his restaurant of choice. Julia always let Liam win, one of the many things he had loved about her.

"I feel that it's important that we choose based on food flavor. Unless you want to scrap the whole dinner thing and just host drinks . . . ," Liam said.

In truth, Julia couldn't care less what sort of food they'd have. She'd pay for ambience over flavor. Not Liam, though.

"What about Italian?" Julia said. "There are nicer, tasteful venues out there. Please—just not Conchita's."

"When you said tasteful, were you referring to food?"

Julia rolled her eyes. "Fine. You can have your favorite shrimp and octopus cocktails while I'll just drown myself in their margaritas. But after dinner, we should transfer to a dance bar for proper drinks!"

"You know that those seafood cocktails are appetizers, right? It's not a beverage," Liam said mockingly while kissing her forehead to appease her from her defeat.

"I don't give a fuck!" Julia was royally pissed.

He gathered she was already imagining the mass quantity of cervezas and carbs the boys would consume and dreading the struggle of getting them up on their feet, much less to a dance club.

• • •

It was a party of twelve and they were all seated together in one long table. Liam had four of his friends there, including Kyle, who arrived late. Julia, statuesque and ever the social butterfly, had made a lot of friends in the three years they were in Oxnard—it had taken a lot of convincing to trim down her guest list. At the end of the day, Julia had invited six girlfriends, including Snow.

Liam got a server to put the velvet proposal ring box on a white plate with a single long-stemmed ivory rose. He had convinced the five-member ensemble to play some lively mariachi music. People had expected him to propose for a while now. Liam wanted to do it at his own pace, and his game plan. This was not necessarily his style. But the element of unexpectedness and the nonconformity made this authentically him.

The distinctively cheerful sound of the guitar, banjo, violin, trumpet, and tambourine started to drown out their conversations. Julia leaned over and asked Liam if someone was celebrating a birthday. When the merriment seemed to approach their space, he watched as she looked to her side to find the five musicians in their big hats and polished-horsemen outfits walking their way to her party.

A server clandestinely placed the white plate with a single long-stemmed ivory rose before Julia, just as Liam had requested. As soon as Julia realized what was transpiring, she made an exaggerated gasp. Liam knew well how this was the kind of reaction the gesture would elicit from his girlfriend. But he had planned for another surprise.

"Oh gosh!" All the girlfriends were equally excited. "Show us the ring!" Loud heckling reverberated in the midst of the jubilant rhythm and vibrato.

When Julia opened the box, it was empty. The guys laughed. The ladies made an even louder gasp. The musicians brusquely stopped. But before he made Julia cry of embarrassment, or made her start hating him for it, Liam was on his knees holding the ring, and spurting out a promise. Ending it with the question of the night, the question of their lifetime—"Will you marry me?"

The mariachi continued with their final piece. As soon as Julia said yes and proceeded to kiss him, a loud cheer loomed behind Liam. It was Kyle, walking toward the group while clapping. He was late. He'd almost missed the dinner.

"Congratulations, bro."

"Thanks. You almost missed the whole thing."

"I know, sorry, dude." Kyle was about to explain but he noticed how Snow was intently listening to his conversation with Liam. He continued with a softer voice. "I almost brought a date tonight. I met someone amazing."

"Yeah." Liam indulged his friend. "How come she's not with you then?"

"She didn't want to crash your party. Too bad you're leaving. I wish you could at least meet her once. I'm serious. I really like her."

Liam shrugged it off as one of Kyle's made-up stories to rationalize his tardiness. Whether it was true or not, it didn't matter to Liam. He had just gotten engaged to Julia.

CHAPTER 17

When the Sun Was Like a Citrus Harvest

"It's easy to fight when everything's right, and you're mad with the thrill and the glory. It's easy to cheer when victory's near, and wallow in fields that are gory. It's a different song when everything's wrong, when you're feeling infernally mortal; When it's ten against one, and hope there is none. Buck up, little soldier."

—Robert W. Service

Kuwait 2009

Nestled between the combative Iraq and the affable Kingdom of Saudi Arabia, Kuwait was a moderate "safe zone." At least more subdued compared to Baghdad. The American intervention during the Iraqi invasion of Kuwait led to a more solid friendship between Kuwait and the US government. For that reason, Kuwait was thought to be the oasis for US soldiers, at least in the Middle East. Sort of an upgrade, a more peaceful and safer option if one had to deploy to this turbulent region of the Persian Gulf, even though Kuwait was supposedly considered one of the driest deserts on earth.

Liam had volunteered to join this assignment. It was not his rotation yet to go on deployment, but he had that dire inclination to escape from Julia. He loved her. And he loved their life together, but he didn't think he was ready to get married yet. Since his proposal, it had been a constant discussion of when, where, then when again. When he heard that it was the guys from Oxnard that he was joining in this detachment in Kuwait—his old buddies like Kyle—Liam readily volunteered. He lied to Julia about this.

"Why are you being deployed? Aren't you supposed to finish this tour on home port?"

"I've been voluntold," Liam rationalized. And Julia didn't question it at all. Julia understood the life of a soldier inasmuch as she got used to the sacrifices a military spouse had to make, even the unofficial ones. She had cried her eyes out, though, for days, as if she had been told he was dying of cancer.

• • •

Kuwait, even in that era, was already an urbanized city of picturesque mosques, high-rise apartments, and avant-garde skyscrapers. It was by no means a vacation spot. But there was some level of inner calm to be found, even in this agitated atmosphere, Liam thought. That inner calm that had slowly left him the past few years. He didn't ponder this much, but he knew it meant he had needed a change, away from Julia. Nothing permanent. He still loved her and cared for the life they had built together. He didn't want to split up, but he welcomed the idea of getting a little breathing space.

• • •

Camp Ali Al Salem was at the outskirts of the city, which meant more sand, less modern civilization. It was also closer to the border separating Kuwait and Iraq. It was relatively quiet, for the most part. Soldiers inside the camp heard a loud boom here and there, although those were few and far between. They had little to complain about, though. The camp had Subway, McDonald's, Taco Bell, Pizza Hut, even Ben & Jerry's. These were just a backup whenever they got tired of the free food at the galley. Full laundry service, their soiled garments came back washed and folded—free of charge. There were internet and phone cafés that could reconnect American soldiers back home. For a fee. This was where he spent most of his low-spirited days, just like the rest of the troops. Or just whenever he missed Julia's voice. Winter weather in Kuwait was milder than back home on the East Coast. He was also happy to be working again among friends. Above all, Liam felt the pressure of getting married off his shoulders.

The galley was basic, as one would expect in the desert. The small space was overlaid with industrial break room tables and chairs. There was always a rush to get a seat during crowded hours. The buffet never strayed from home-cooked comfort food, except when on Fridays the command would go all out with surf and turf.

More than the food, it was the conversations that made the galley the place to be. With no opportunity to leave the base except on missions, one made the most of what one could get. Hence, the galley was a prime spot.

Everyone was relaxed whenever they were in front of a warm meal, so chatter was always light. Except when there was a troll at the table.

"Hey man, can you pass me the salt please." Liam knew that Kyle prided himself on the fact that he was tough looking and burly, but also on the fact that his manners were always impeccable. It was easy to like him. Everyone did. Although from time to time, his politeness was the object of ridicule for clowns like Pete. But Kyle was a fighter, a real trooper. Not one to back down easily.

As Kyle dusted salt on his food, Pete said, "Easy on the salt. Those biceps may all be from water retention."

"Oh Pete, you make me miss my wife. Don't waste that sweet talk on me though. Do it with your girl, okay?" Kyle's knack for sarcasm, by a long shot, handled banter better than anyone.

"How's your wife, Kyle?" One of the guys tried to change the flow of conversation.

"She's alright, man. Few more weeks till I become a dad. I just wish I could be with her for that."

"Childbirth's overrated. Trust me, you should feel lucky you won't be in that room. You might not ever look at your wife the same way again, after." Just like most of the guys at the table, Pete was a petty officer second class, typical rank for a seventh-year career. But unlike most of them, Pete was a first-class bonehead.

"You're a classic douche, Pete," Liam managed to say while he was busy breaking up the crab legs.

"Well, have you been married or got a girl knocked up? Then you wouldn't know it, Lee."

"First of all, my name is Liam, not Lee. Second . . ." Liam paused, then snickered as he thought there was no sense getting riled up over this.

Someone else picked up on Liam's thoughts. "There's no point in that, because Pete is hopeless." It was the best everyone could do to end the chatter. Leave Pete out as if he was not even at the table.

"What I want to know is how you can enjoy those crab legs?"

Liam scoffed at himself too. He devoured all the seafood while the cowboy-soldiers persisted on the grilled red meat.

"Hey. I don't know how you guys go through life without tasting the sweetness of these crab legs," Liam said.

"By the way . . ." Liam almost forgot asking this favor, being too consumed with his lunch. "Can someone swap schedules with me this Sunday? I'm on night duty but I need to call home." Julia had been acting unreasonable lately. He expected successions of phone calls and wasting a couple of hours of his time going back and forth to queue up for another stab at the phone until his girlfriend was appeased.

"Well, don't expect me to do it. I might be working the day shift with you anyway." Pete was never the type to give out favors.

"I'll do it. I can call my wife any hour of the day."

"Thanks, Kyle."

· · ·

Liam woke up bright and early on Sunday. Way too early, as a matter of fact. He had trouble sleeping whenever Julia was going though one of her cycles—the impatient fiancée, doubtful of their future together.

The sky was surprising, its colors delectable—the amalgamated skyline of fresh limes and bluish berries, which were mirrored in the color of the sea, and the brightened, ripest sun illuminating like a citrus harvest, the pulp of a grapefruit laid against the skin of a tangerine—unlike most days when the sandy grounds and the pile of clouds were impossible to tell apart—both lifeless in murky gray.

It would have been like any ordinary day. Pete and Liam were tasked to unload supplies from the C-17 cargo aircraft that just landed the camp. Pete, right away, assigned himself to be the one taking down the shipments off the plane, which left Liam with doing the heavier lifting of the task. Liam didn't mind walking back and forth. He preferred being under the bright-colored skyline than be holed up at the tail end of the cargo.

Both started with the heap of smaller, more manageable boxes. They were waiting for two more to help with the unloading of the larger freight. Liam sent them to get the forklift and a caster dolly.

He had been moving small boxes to a nearby pile instead of standing frivolously waiting for the two guys to come back. As it happened, he saw one package for Kyle while he quickly perused through the stack of parcels. When Liam saw Kyle passing by, presumably on his way to the galley or the internet café, he instinctively flagged his friend. As Kyle walked in Liam's direction, a sudden explosion came in between, separating them. It was the loudest boom anyone in the camp had ever heard. It would also be the last sound Liam would ever receive.

Liam had never experienced sinking into deep water as if he was drowning, but he imagined the experience was the same— suffocating, like someone squeezing the life out of him. He was overcome by a strong force that encased his whole being, even in an open space, and then was flung off in mid-air, landing without mercy. Even then he should have been thankful for being blown away to a safer distance, away from the fireball of fuming flames that consumed Pete instantaneously. The package Liam was holding—meant for Kyle—had somehow saved him from absolute destruction. It miraculously served as a protective buffer between his lobbed body and the rigid earth as he plummeted like dust settling to the ground, without a sound.

• • •

Hours passed, then days. Liam was lost in a black hole, as if submerged in the deepest chasm of the Mariana Trench. When he hovered back to existence, his first thought was how pissed Julia must have been, waiting by the phone for a call that never went through. She had no idea that he'd gotten knocked out and tossed around like a pebble. Because she was only a secondary in case of emergency, she would have to hear from Liam's mother instead of getting the news firsthand. Because she was already worried about their future, Liam's new state would surely increase that angst.

Liam had suffered considerably but not as much as Pete. Or Pete's family. "Could you tell me if he died instantly?" Liam struggled to ask. "Was he mercifully spared from the burning flame or the punctures of the blast?" No one could decisively answer. At the same time, Liam couldn't hear anyone who attempted to explain.

There would be more tests to determine if his hearing loss was temporary. Or how profound. There would be more routine examinations to determine his recovery—physically and psychologically.

• • •

Investigators came to his room as often as the medical team. They had just as many questions as his doctors did. It didn't matter that

Liam was so clueless and besieged—that he felt just as dead inside as Pete. Their concern was piecing together the incident.

"Why do you feel like you were responsible?" they asked him. This line of questioning was ruthless. Although Liam was no longer able to hear the tone in their voice, the circumspection in the words as he read the interrogations was appalling.

"I didn't say responsible. I said I felt partly at fault." He imagined he was probably shouting whenever he replied, because he saw some stunned facial expressions. "Look, this is all unfamiliar to me. Not being able to hear my own voice is strange."

"No need to apologize. We just have a few more questions if you want to continue reading the other paper." One female investigator handed over a smaller note, which she hurriedly wrote, posing this to be her way of being considerate.

"Sorry, I'm thrown off by all this," Liam responded. "Someone died. He was someone I knew. I was close to being blown up myself, so forgive me if I don't feel too neat about surviving this tragedy. The way everyone expects me to feel." Liam was frustrated. "I've been racking my brain trying to remember things. Pete wanted to unload and stay inside the plane. Kyle walked toward me, toward the plane. I'd told him he had a package, flagged him to come my way. Knowing he's in critical condition is something I'm having trouble reconciling. On that one, I was sort of responsible."

"Again, if you had no prior knowledge that there would be an explosion, why would you blame yourself?" As he floundered within the newly silent world, the investigators and the psychiatrist all *sounded* the same. He wanted to be left alone.

It was survivor's guilt that had delayed his recovery. He hadn't cared much for Pete when he was alive. He hated him more now for being dead. And what kind of a friend was he to drag Kyle into this?

Everyone kept saying he should share his sentiments to help with his healing. How could he? For one thing, he had completely lost his hearing. He struggled with communication. Liam thought if he couldn't hear, he might as well stop talking.

CHAPTER 18

When You're Never the Same Again

"If you can't be a highway, then just be a trail. If you can't be the sun, be a star; It isn't by size that you win or you fail—Be the best of whatever you are!"

—Douglas Malloch

"You lost some. But you gained more," his mother said to Liam. It was his mother's new favorite expression. "Look at where your life has taken you." Her mantra, a constant reminder of his solemn oath to the path he chose to march through. For the most part, and on most days, it was true. It was in fact a turning point that he didn't know he needed.

Eight months after the accident in Kuwait, Liam and Julia broke up. Liam lost his hearing, then lost Julia too. But she didn't leave him voluntarily. She left because Liam had told her to get on with her life without him.

"Hey, I think we need to talk." He'd found the courage to set his girlfriend free from his promise. He saw no point in being miserable together, and he often felt miserable. "I feel like falling into the lowest cavity and I don't want to drag you with me." It was the least he could do for her, the kindest kind of love he could give her.

Julia tried to offer reasons as to why they should work on their relationship. But the communication barrier made it all worse. He couldn't hear her. Rather, he refused to hear anything further. Liam simply said, "It's time for us to part ways. I've known this for years. Even before I left for Kuwait."

There came a moment of weakness when he wanted to take back all the harsh things he'd said about their relationship. Liam wanted to win her back. Except that, unexpectedly, she had moved on faster than he had anticipated. Julia, as her track record indicated, was usually indecisive, a fickle mind. The day they broke up, she left him a short note. Her words were uncharacteristically clear and uncompromising. "You're going to regret this, Liam. Mark my words." She was right. Liam grieved over every word.

The first time Liam waited for a chance to talk again to Julia, he spent two hours in his car, parked a few spots down from where Julia's car was parked at her work. Julia came out with a couple of girlfriends. They were giggling at something someone had said while walking in the parking lot, presumably on their way to after-work drinks. Liam lost the nerve to show himself to Julia. It felt intrusive and rude to approach her then.

He tried once more. When Julia came out of her work building, she was on the phone. She appeared happy. Then she walked further away from her car and got into someone else's car. Liam didn't need to probe deeper to know that an ambush meet-up that night was a foolish coup.

As a final effort, Liam showed up at her parents' house. Her mother was pleased to see him until her uneasiness started to manifest itself. She wrote down what felt like his life sentence on a piece of paper. "Julia has already moved out. She moved in with her new boyfriend."

• • •

In the long run, the accident revealed more things about himself than he would have known if things had stayed the same in his life. It was a process, but everything started to fall into place. Liam found the motivation to make more than what was expected of him. He started to listen from within when the outside noise stopped coming in. If only to know that his inner voice had so much more to say. Liam heard himself as soon as he accepted his fate.

He moved back home to Louisville and stayed with his mother after he gave up on winning back Julia.

"You can lead a horse to water, but you can't make it drink. It's all on you, Liam," his mother told him.

• • •

Like anyone who had to start over, it didn't start out easy. Because he had many years as a hearing person, Liam had trouble learning how to communicate without his words. It was similar to having a numb mouth after a local anesthetic injection. He watched himself in the mirror, moving his mouth, but he couldn't quite feel the movement he made. He saw it but he didn't feel it. It was the same thing as speaking out his words. He knew what he said but he couldn't hear himself. There was that missing link. A disconnect.

In the beginning, Liam was skeptical about learning to sign. He reasoned to his mother, "I could talk. I could read. It should be enough to get by." And for the most part, it was enough.

The disconnect was beyond not being able to hear. It was more about not having a meaningful purpose. His life with Julia was neither happy nor sad. It was average, right in the middle. After the accident, he went through a darker time. It was then that he began to be more grateful for every little perk. He learned to appreciate even trivial things. He worked hard to be happy.

Liam started attending a sign language school and took up some night classes at a community college. Because most of the professors didn't expect to teach a Deaf student, they practically exempted Liam from all tasks. They were mostly embarrassed to admit that the courses were developed for hearing students only.

From that point on, the nagging desire grew in him to build a system that might help Deaf kids who struggled with learning because of the lack of fundamental skills in communication.

One morning while Liam was reading a book, his mom went up to him with a portable chalkboard. She wrote, "I'm off to my cooking class. Your lunch is in the crockpot."

"Mom . . . ," Liam said, stopping his mother from taking off. "Why do you go to cooking class when you have a collection of recipe books?"

Liam's mom went back to the chalkboard to erase her message, then wrote a new one. "Because I need someone to demonstrate what I see in my recipe books."

It was like a lightbulb moment for Liam as soon as he read his mom's response. He smiled before proceeding to ask his mom, "How would you feel about losing your TV room?"

Liam's mom gave a puzzled look and shrugged her shoulders. Without asking his reason, she wrote as a reply to him, "Whatever you need, son."

Perhaps it was the word "demonstrate," or the chalkboard, but Liam spent the next two months transforming his mom's living room into a small classroom, with a large chalkboard on one wall and an equally large ASL alphabet chart posted across the other wall. He had two Deaf students, both boys from the same church his mother attended. The boys' hearing parents and Liam's mom also attended the weekend workshops. Whenever a new student asked to join, Liam required that a parent attend the class too. He reasoned that the student would be encouraged to learn ASL if a family member also understood and communicated using ASL.

Then the workshop became a school. As he saw the progress he was making with his students, he turned his program into five days a week. He offered it to a larger number and with a wider age range. Slowly his school grew from a one-man, part-time job to a venture with twenty employees, most of whom had either partial or profound hearing loss.

From a struggling business that ate up most of the disability pay he received from the US Navy, Liam turned it around to a fully operational school with a long list of patrons that allowed the school to subsidize the cost of education for most of its students. Liam couldn't categorically say that it was a nonprofit, because he profited a lot from this—he had gained a purpose-driven life. The friendships of the students and their families. A supportive community. A culture he had never imagined merging himself into. A financially stable life. His inner voice. His mother's pride.

· · ·

The school—The Peter Kingston Center for the Deaf—was set up like one big library where silence was encouraged, as well as reading. The hallway was lined with multiple tables for group studies. On both sides were private rooms reserved for classes and forums. The second floor was the resource center where the learning materials and staff offices were located. Outside the library were three separate structures, which he slowly added each year. During the first year, he built an outdoor sports quad for basketball and volleyball. In the second year, he built a music hall with state-of-the-art sound systems that were calibrated to blast off heart-pumping beats. For its third year, the school welcomed an auditorium for special events like offering students silent or foreign movies—anything with reputable subtitles.

Liam had dedicated his life to this school, and the dream had become a reality.

· · ·

It had been two months since Liam got back from Manila. He had been feeling miserable, almost regretful of his decision. When he caught a glimpse of the wallpaper on Kate's phone—Kyle, Kate, and their son—his immediate thought was to stay away from her. It didn't feel right to be with her. She was Kyle's.

Liam had heard about what happened to their son. He almost flew to California to attend the funeral. He would have met Kate then. At her son's memorial service. At her worst nightmare.

Kyle and Liam had remained friends. Not the kind that communicated often. It was mostly during Thanksgiving or Christmas when they would send an email greeting and a short update. Liam went back to the old emails they had exchanged—he was trying to get a glimpse into the state of Kate and Kyle's life together.

• • •

December 18, 2014

Kyle,

I heard about your son. So sorry to hear this news. I know your family will pull through the toughest time. Be good to your wife. Wishing you a Happy Holidays just the same. Hang in there.

Liam

• • •

Reply to Liam:

January 12, 2015

Great to hear from you. Yup it's been tough on us. Christmas was rough. Are you still single? There's a part of me that can't blame you now. Marriage is hard, bro.

Kyle

Liam was interrupted by someone popping in at the door. His mind had drifted far too long. A pile of paper clips he reflexively unbent then twisted to different shapes was now spread out in front of him. Lisa, his office manager, looked at them curiously before she signed that it was time. They were having a small celebratory program to mark the four-year anniversary of the school. Every year, Liam presented a slideshow for the benefit of the hearing and the nonhearing. The whole program was signed, so each hearing guest was provided an audio device and an earphone. Liam opted to change it this year. He wanted to talk, give a speech, while Noah, one of the students who read through a teleprompter, signed for the audience.

He took a deep breath. Not only was this his first time to deliver a speech, it was also the first time to use his voice in school.

"Good afternoon. I decided I should change the way I presented this year. I have a voice, so I thought, why not use it. For most people, the way they communicated was never a point of consideration. It was always what was practiced in the community. That's how dialects prevailed, based on geography. Culture also dictated our manner of speech. That's how the term 'politically correct' was coined."

Liam paused as he waited for Noah to catch up with his signing.

"As we all know, not all communications are through spoken words. We don't have to be hearing to engage in conversations. We don't need to be speaking to voice our thoughts."

Liam paused again to scan the room. He saw his proud mother, his younger sister, and an older brother. He located his staff in the audience, who all looked straight at him encouragingly. He nodded at the school's benefactors and located his students, whose lips were pressed into thin lines while their parents stood with creased brows, perhaps apprehensive of where his speech was going.

"I just looked at each one of you and saw on your faces varied reactions to the opening of my speech. This is because a message, even when delivered the same way, can come across differently to different receivers. Which brings me to my focus for this year—the perils of miscommunication. Quite often, we read the same passage as the person next to us, yet we understand it in our own way. And when one says 'our own way,' it can mean a variety of things—it could range from north to south, always to never, love to hate. A message that sounds as benign as 'I don't care' to mean that you don't have a preference can easily be construed as aggressive. Then these two different interpretations lead to opposite endings. Believe me, it's possible. And it happens. That's why there are sets of standards for systems, for how we measure things. Formulas for math. Core principles for how we teach English and ASL."

Liam paused again and turned to Noah, the student sharing the stage with him. Liam signed to ask if he was doing all right or if he needed to slow down.

"By the way, thank you, Noah, for doing an excellent job here. I have full confidence that if there's any miscommunication, it's them—not you. Never blame the messenger." Short pause. "Here's a fun fact. In some very remote villages and mountain ranges in Africa, Turkey, and other parts of the world where technology has not invaded, how do you think people communicate for urgent messages that need to be transmitted? Where phones are not an option, or email, or even a radio transmitter? Think about it. When traveling from one point to the next just to speak in person would take days, how do you think individuals communicate?"

Short pause.

"There are communities around the world that use whistling— yes, the villagers whistle—to send urgent messages, such as a simple call for help, or to warn friends of imminent danger, or to announce death. This is known as the bird language. Some call it the bat language. They don't use words. They use codes. Sounds that can reverberate. Why did I bring this up? Lucky for us, we don't have to rely on this system. Or for that matter, we don't live in remote areas. But what I wanted to emphasize is how privileged we are that we have found our niche. Something that works for us. We found our own way to communicate among our family, as a community, as a culture. That is why we make it a point to celebrate each one of you—from our generous benefactors, to supportive families, hardworking teachers, and exceptional students, because each one of you helped bridge the gap of disparity—the disconnect. Otherwise, the lack of basic communication skills could leave us all exposed. Vulnerable. At a disadvantage."

Everyone in the auditorium raised their palms forward and struck them in motion as a way of applause. And afterward, everyone Liam bumped into in the hallway clasped their hands together to indicate "congratulations" on his speech. While he beamed with pride on the success of the event, Liam couldn't help but wonder about Kate. Beneath his pretense that it was wrong for them to be together, his inner voice had been saying the opposite. He had been feeling conflicted, at odds with what he believed to be the decent thing to do. Even now, here, where he should be able to focus on the present moment, he was distracted. His thoughts lingered on her.

Kate had stopped replying to his messages. Clearly, there was miscommunication that led them to this state. It was not lost on him how ironic his speech was about the perils of miscommunication. Her last message gave him the impression that she felt used, and she thought that he'd only wanted to fool around. He regretted the way he handled things between them. If nothing else, he would like for her to know that it wasn't what she thought it was. That she wasn't a fling, and that the weekend together probably meant more to him than it did to her.

CHAPTER 19

When You've
Been Split in Two

"For the hearts that break in silence, with a sorrow all unknown.
For those who need companions, yet walk their ways alone."
—Ella Wheeler Wilcox

There was a knot inside me. I was back in this crater of anxiety as I stepped out of the plane that took me straight home from Manila to Los Angeles. Back to my life, my reality. This time I carried an added baggage with me—thoughts of Liam.

Kyle was waiting for me when I arrived at LAX. As soon as he saw me, Kyle went up to hug me tightly, as if I had been lost and was now found. I was perplexed as to how I felt about this. We both had decided to get a divorce, so I was a little uneasy about his gestures. I had only told my mom about my flight back home and hadn't expected Kyle to show up at the airport. Or to receive a welcome-back hug.

"Are you hungry? We can stop for food before we drive home." Kyle glanced at me longer than he needed to as he waited for my response. The traffic was slow moving. It gave Kyle more chances to assess my impassiveness.

"No, I'm good."

"Are you sure? With this traffic, we could be getting home late. I don't think we have food in the house."

"You can drop me off at my mom's."

"To eat?"

"No, Kyle. For me to stay at."

"Kate . . ."

"What now, Kyle? What changed? Are we little kids that easily change their minds?'

"No." Kyle sounded agitated. "I didn't expect you to take off the way that you did. I was hoping we could talk more . . . talk things through. We really have to sit down and decide our future."

"You sounded sure when you asked for a divorce."

"And I was . . . at that time." There was tentativeness in his voice. "I don't know how I feel now."

"When are you moving to Gulfport?"

"Next year. June."

I took this in as our reality. Moving from one station to another, separation due to deployment—these had always been on the horizon when I married a soldier. I had reconciled this as part of the package when we started our little family. But we didn't have a son anymore. Did we still need to be a family?

"Please talk to me, Kate."

Believe me, Kyle, I so badly wanted to say. *It's better I keep my thoughts to myself for now.*

· · ·

Cold air greeted me as I opened the front door. Cold air that numbed my troubled heart as I walked back into the house I shared with Kyle. The house that my son never got to see. The house that we tried to put our lives back together in as we struggled to move forward as a childless couple. It was our place of safety, our sanctuary from the pain. Only, it didn't do much. Instead, it opened our eyes to the truth. We were broken as soon as our son left our lives. We could only heal as individuals, not as a family.

"I'm staying in the guest bedroom." This was a three-bedroom house. The master, guestroom, and Willy's room. I felt safest in the second room.

"You can stay in our room and I'll move to the guest room." We were both plodding across unknown terrain. We needed time and space, whether we admitted it openly or not.

"Please, Kyle. Let's make it easy on ourselves. I already said I'm staying there—let's leave it at that."

"Okay." Kyle let out a heavy sigh, which I could have easily construed as protest, or frustration. Anger. Or ache. But I needed to learn not to presume. Not with Kyle. Not with Liam. And not with my own feelings. "Can I at least help you move things you'll need in that room?"

"Thank you." It was all I could manage to tell him. For now.

I was tossing and turning in my bed, finding the right balance to rest my tired self. After a few hours of failed attempts, I gave up and turned on the light. I had never finished that book I bought at the Tokyo airport bookshop.

Two hours into reading, I came across a handwritten note from Liam.

"I can't imagine a world where meeting you was as meaningless as sharing trivial details about myself, such as how I used to listen to Snoop Dogg. Have dinner with me at least? Sorry I scribbled on your book. I didn't think this through."

I placed the book down next to me on the bed. I turned my body to bury my face on my pillow. With my mouth covered to conceal any sound, I slowly liberated a tormented wail.

• • •

For the next couple of months, Kyle and I were like roommates sharing a house. Separate spaces, separate lives. We survived Thanksgiving, thankfully. Kyle left to see his parents while I stayed with my mom and stepdad.

"Kate, tell us the truth. What's happening between you and Kyle?"

When I said I survived Thanksgiving, it didn't mean that the dinner proceeded without difficulty. My mom got on with her grilling early. Not the meat, but me. Even before Barry could slice through the turkey.

"We're still figuring things out. He's moving to Gulfport in seven months."

"Oh, I thought that was no longer happening." My mom was telling herself more than she was telling me.

"How did you even know about Gulfport?" I avoided discussing anything about my marriage with her since I had returned from my trip, to the point of bringing Kyle over with me to dinner the few times, when my excuses were no longer acceptable. On the barely bright side, at least my mom was less meddling whenever Kyle was around.

"I knew that was how the divorce talk started. When I asked Kyle to bring you back home, he explained to me why you abruptly left. Because frankly, I was so confused over why you would take off like that. It didn't make sense to me." My mom said this without a censor. She had no idea how deceived I felt to hear this. I had thought all along that it was just Kyle who had asked me to come back home. I was foolish not to suspect that my mother urged him to send that message.

I felt my blood run cold. This little revelation bruised me once more. I felt cheated somehow. That simple text from Kyle, to come home . . . It was not a plea from my husband. It was from my mom. She unknowingly pulled me back to a life I had almost escaped from unscathed.

I stood up and went to the powder room. I couldn't cry in front of my mom because she would only howl louder than I did. Nobody could blame a mother for wanting her child back.

Slumped on the floor with my arms embracing my folded knees, I let my tears go. Where no one could see. My heart thumped in anger. My mind squabbled in regret. I had almost freed myself from this miserable marriage if not for that one text which made me doubt my actions. Which took me back here. And now on this floor. With my mother outside the door. Banging. Asking me to come out. Pleading. Crying. Just as I was.

I didn't confront Kyle about the text. It wouldn't have changed much.

. . .

There were nights when Kyle would invite me to share a glass of wine with him. One of us would end up more miserable, the other one frustrated. Or one of us angrier, the other one lonelier. The scenarios varied but none of them were helpful. Or encouraging.

"Why will you not let me touch you, Kate? Is there someone else?" Kyle had asked this so many times. Whether he was sober or drunk. In passing, or during a meal. Or even through a text. I didn't know what had been stopping me from telling Kyle about Liam. It was not like I was afraid to lose Kyle. I had already lost him, in the moment I had kissed Liam. Or before then, rather. I lost my husband as soon as I lost my son.

I kept the idea of Liam in me because I didn't know what it was that we had. I thought I did, but then it ended with me doubting him. He was hovering in my head, in my heart. But it was more of a muddle of uncertainty and foolish elation, which was drowning me, keeping me wheezing for air. And so, I put memories of him away too. Just as I did with the memories of my son, my father, and my marriage.

. . .

It had been three months since I had returned from Manila. The neighbors had already started hanging holiday lights on their eaves and front yard trees, and setting out colorful tinsel, inflatable snowmen, and animated reindeers. Just as in years past, the holiday spirit skipped us. Or we skipped it.

Kyle was already making dinner when I got home from work. He had made pizza out of naan bread, topped with smoked mozzarella pearls, cherry tomatoes, arugula, and a drizzle of olive oil and fig balsamic.

"Thank you for dinner. I'm off tomorrow, so it will be my turn."

"I actually meant to tell you that an old buddy is in town visiting. I hope you don't mind that I invited him over tomorrow. I can get takeout instead. He's just by himself."

"Oh, no worries. I can make something for the three of us."

"Great. Thanks, Kate." Gone were terms of endearment like "babe."

· · ·

Have you ever had that crazy moment when there were too many things clouding your mind that your brain got scrambled? As soon as Kyle's guest walked in, all things went south. Short of dropping a serving bowl full of pasta, I was in disarray. At least in my head. Because in reality, I was immobilized. I stood frozen as I watched Liam come near me to offer a handshake. I managed to bring the pasta bowl down on the counter to receive Liam's hand.

I was confused. I was thrilled. I was shocked. I only snapped out of my rattled head when I realized that I was throwing the cupcakes away in the trash bin instead of arranging them on a platter.

"Kate! Kate!" Kyle cajoled me to stop from mindlessly tossing them in the trash. Just in time to save the last cupcake.

Kyle took Liam to the living room and went back to the kitchen. "So how are we going to do this?" Kyle said this more to himself than to me. Kyle paced back and forth at the kitchen island. He then turned to me and said, "Kate, my friend lost his hearing in Kuwait.

We were together in that accident. He lost his hearing. How do you think we should talk tonight?"

I turned to one of the drawers and handed Kyle a pen and a notepad. Kyle went back to the couch and I heard Liam say, "Sure, that will work."

I was deliberately slow in arranging the dinner table to buy time. I couldn't believe the derision. They were together in Kuwait. He was that friend who sent us the kite book that Willy loved. He was that friend whom we named our son after. What sort of a cruel joke was this? I was angry. But to whom I should direct my anger at was beyond me.

As I set the plates, the silver, the rigatoni bolognese, the salad, and the garlic bread on the table, I glanced at Liam to make sure this was real. The thing with Liam, he knew right away when someone was watching him. His eyes darted at me as soon as I looked his way.

Kyle turned around too, perhaps after seeing how Liam's eyes shifted toward the dinner table. "Oh, it's ready." Kyle stood and motioned his hand as a way of an invitation.

Kyle took the end of the rectangle table, while Liam and I were seated across from each other.

"Thank you for having me, Kate." Liam's voice melted me once again.

Kyle waved his hand, presumably to mean "it was nothing," or "no need to say that."

I passed the salad to Liam first, as he was our guest. Not because he was my favorite person. Or that I missed him. Or that I was glad to have unknowingly made this dinner for him.

"Please, Kate, you should go first." Liam smiled graciously, but I could only speculate as to the ruckus that roiled within him, just as it did within me.

Kyle started using the notepad. "Why are you back in Oxnard?"

"Just visiting."

I jumped on the question, interrupting Liam and surprising Kyle and myself. "He's been here before?" My question was for Liam, but I somehow directed it to Kyle.

"Yeah, we were stationed together here. Remember that night we met, when I invited you to a dinner after the movie, but you declined? It was a farewell dinner for him and his girlfriend. It was actually the night he proposed to her," Kyle explained.

I made sure that Liam noticed how my brows creased. Then, as I raised one of them after hearing the word girlfriend, Liam said curiously, "Okay, tell me all of that, please. Write it down, Kyle. I don't read lips."

I grabbed the notepad from Kyle and wrote for him. "I was surprised to learn that you lived here before." I pulled the notepad up to show Liam. He smiled while nodding so I went back to the notepad and wrote the other half of the information Kyle had eagerly shared with me. "And that we almost met at the proposal dinner for your girlfriend."

"Huh . . ." Liam quit smiling. "Oh, it was more of a going-away for me." Liam said this defensively.

"You should have seen that proposal," Kyle said. "It was hilarious. That dude had taken the ring out so Julia, his girlfriend then, was stunned to open an empty box."

"Why are you excluding him from the conversation?" I said to Kyle. "You know your friend can't hear." It was hard to mask my irritation.

"Oh, I'm sorry." Kyle's happy mood suddenly went sour. "I just remembered how funny it was, so I wanted to share it with you. And the fact that you almost went with me that night."

"What's happening again?" Liam interrupted.

Kyle motioned his hand sideways as he said "nothing." With my thumb bent and the rest of my fingers spread out, I moved that hand from my mouth to a sideways motion to properly say "ignore it." Liam appeared pleasantly surprised that I had learned to sign. He signed "thank you" to me. Kyle was visibly slighted with how I berated him. He didn't seem to notice that I was signing, that I knew how to sign.

I took the notepad and asked, "When did you arrive?"

"Yesterday morning." Liam responded with his voice.

I wrote a follow-up. "How long are you staying?"

"A few days."

Kyle stood up to grab drinks. My breathing became more labored as we were left alone at the table. I had to avoid Liam's piercing gaze, so I grabbed the bread tray and offered it to him. Instead of taking a piece of bread, he took the tray out of my hand while slightly touching the tips of my fingers.

Kyle joined the table with two bottles of Heineken light. I turned to Kyle and suggested, "We have tall glasses for beer."

"Right." Kyle left the table again.

"I think I've seen you somewhere before, Kate," Liam stated for both Kyle and me to hear.

I gave Liam a peering reaction. I tilted my head to the side, curious as to where this was going. I didn't know what his intentions were, but I was not afraid of anything.

"Oh really." Kyle answered for me as he walked back to the table and handed a glass for Liam.

I motioned my index finger from my mouth with the rest of

fingers closed on a fist then pulled it away from me while bending that index finger to a closed fist while lifting the thumb and pinkie as I mouthed the word "really."

Kyle watched me sign and asked in a tone of disbelief, "When did you learn sign language?"

Before I replied to Kyle, I wrote to Liam. "Kyle was asking about when I learned to sign."

Liam nodded and said, "It's a nice surprise to meet someone who can sign."

Kyle didn't even acknowledge Liam's remark. He seemed bothered so I asked him, "Why do you look upset, Kyle?"

"No, I'm sorry. Not upset," Kyle said, immediately changing his unsettled expression with a forced smile. "Taken aback perhaps. Wondering how I never knew. What made you decide to learn that?"

I wrote my reply instead of speaking it out. I showed the paper to Kyle then to Liam.

"I just started learning ASL. I met someone who inspired me to learn."

"Who?" Kyle asked even before I could show the notepad to Liam.

"Just a friend. A regular at the bakeshop." I wrote this for Liam's sake, so that he knew what was going on. "I told Kyle I learned ASL for a friend, a regular at the bakeshop."

"That's where I knew you from," Liam said.

Kyle looked at him and nodded. He took the notepad and wrote. "Yes. The muffins you used to bring at work. Kate works there."

It was my turn again to be surprised. "What?"

Liam read me clearly because he offered immediately, "My ex-girlfriend used to buy from that bakeshop. We never met, because I usually stayed in the car. But I've seen you at the store. That's why I said you looked familiar. My ex-girlfriend always bought more than what we could eat, so I took the extras to work. Kyle even asked where I got them from, but I never told him."

"Huh." That was all I could manage to say. *What a bizarre coincidence!*

"Before I forget, I always thought it was rude to go to a friend's house empty-handed, so I brought this for you both as a gift." As expected, Liam handed it to me, not to Kyle.

I mouthed "thank you" as I raised my open palms facing inward to touch my lip then motioned it away.

"You can unwrap it if you want," Liam said encouragingly.

Kyle was about to motion his hands again presumably to say "there's no need to" when I interrupted to say under my breath, "Yes, I'd love to see what this is."

I gently unwrapped his gift, not wanting to tear off the wrapping paper indiscriminately. I suppressed a gasp, not wanting to make Kyle even more inquisitive. It was a framed photograph of that pristine white oval tub filled with water and set outdoors among young bamboo trees. From the bathroom at the sanctuary.

"Is that a bathtub?" Kyle blurted out as he took the frame from my hand and examined the gift. Kyle looked at Liam curiously, so he felt obligated to explain.

"I'm into photography—still photography. Hopefully there's a corner somewhere you can place that in. To remind you that I was once a guest in your house."

"Of course." Kyle motioned a thumbs-up. "Talk about a picture being worth a thousand words," he added mockingly, under his breath.

It was indeed worth a thousand words. It brought a memory together—the looseness of my decisions that gave me the fleeting joy of freedom, against the perils of exposing myself to heartache again. In the end, that freedom took me to a place of doubt but also longing and hope, and pushed me to go on.

"Please excuse me. I need to do something upstairs." I stood up, almost choking. I could feel my face go pink and hot.

"Are you okay, Kate?" Kyle asked as he held my hand. Liam's eyes were now on Kyle's hand.

I nodded as I pulled away from his grip. I saw Kyle scribbling something on the notepad, presumably to explain why I had left the table. And even without looking, I could feel Liam's eyes follow me as I rushed upstairs. I went to my room, locked the door, and buried my face in the pillow. I couldn't fathom the situation.

It didn't take long for Liam to send me a message on my phone. "Are you okay?"

"Was any of it real?" A question I had been meaning to ask him since we separated. I had been tempted to ask for so long that I felt liberated to finally have this chance.

"All of it was real. Please believe me."

"When did you know that I was married to Kyle?"

"That morning you left. I accidentally saw your phone flashing while you were sleeping on the daybed. I saw the wallpaper, a photo of you with Kyle and your son."

"Was that why you sent me home?"

"I didn't mean it that way. I regret how it turned out. Please come back downstairs."

When I joined Kyle and Liam back at the table, I noticed the amount of beer that Kyle had already consumed. He was not wasted, but was no longer legally allowed to drive. So I wrote, "I think Kyle had too much to drink. I'll drive you back to your hotel. Please let me know when you're ready."

"Oh shoot," Kyle managed to say. "I'm sorry, Kate. I'll stay behind and clean up here. He's a friend. He's cool."

"I'm not worried," I told Kyle.

Because I was the one driving, Liam spent the entire ride asking questions that I could answer by nodding or shaking my head.

"Are you still mad at me?"

I tentatively shook my head. I knew this to be true.

"Are you divorced?"

I regrettably shook my head again.

"Are you upset that I showed up at your house? I guess I was desperate."

I let that one pass in one ear and out the other. Part of me was also desperate to see him again.

"Are you happy?"

I ignored Liam. I kept both of my hands on the steering wheel and held my head straight, careful not to move it so it would not be mistaken for either a yes or a no.

Once we reached the parking lot of the hotel, Liam looked at me. He gently tried to move my chin so we could be facing each other.

"So, what does it mean? Are you back together?"

I brought my thumb, index, and middle finger together, the tips of all three fingers touching twice to say "no." But it was hard to explain why—to him and to myself—so I kept my gaze down.

Liam pulled my face up and asked, "What about us? How are we?"

I shook my head.

"No, we're not okay? Or no, we're done?" Liam clarified.

I replied through text. "No, there's no us."

"Why?"

I replied again through text. "Because you were right to push me away and send me back to Kyle. There could never be an 'us.' Not with the kind of history that you and Kyle had."

We sat in silence. Lost for words. Uncertain how to make things right. Because we couldn't. And we both knew it. My phone started flashing for an incoming call from Kyle. I was about to answer it when Liam gently took my face so I could receive his kiss. It was a tender, short kiss. Then he said, "Goodbye, Kate." An unbearable tightness filled my throat. I was left with no words.

I watched Liam get out of my car, walking away without looking back. I had hoped that it would be more like watching a sunset, when the sun disappears into the night but with expectations of it rising again in the morning. That it would not feel this grave. That it would not feel like I had died again.

CHAPTER 20

When Cats Run Out of Lives

"I've heard it in the chilliest land. And on the strangest sea;
Yet, never, in extremity; It asked a crumb of me."

—Emily Dickinson

Shakespeare, in *Romeo and Juliet*, wrote "Good king of cats, nothing but one of your nine lives." The myth of cats having nine lives was prevalent in ancient Egypt. One Egyptian sun god had gone to the underworld and given birth to eight other gods, which explained the belief in nine lives. Chinese culture also believed in this—nine was a lucky number for them.

Like a cat with nine lives, I could very well have used up a few, at least spiritually speaking. The first time I heard the prognosis, acute lymphoblastic leukemia, there was a part of me that died right at the doctor's visit. Sinking in the sand is worse than just being buried, because as you sink, you gasp for air. There are moments of false hope, when you feel as though you might survive it. When I heard the doctor telling me how sick my son was, I wanted to break away from that moment, go back in time, to amend what I'd done wrong. Challenge it. Fight it. In my mind, there must have been something I did as a mother that played a role in my son's illness. Whatever it was, I would undo it, or at least I had hope that I could.

I remembered my reaction to the doctor's prognosis. It was as if he was the bad guy. Someone had to be the bad guy. "Do you have to be mean about it?" was the thing that my brain managed to spit out, as if the doctor was attacking me, trying to hurt me with his medical finding.

Kyle stopped me from my outburst. "Kate!" he hissed, while the doctor simultaneously said, "Excuse me?"

• • •

As one would expect, I died inside when my son Willy passed away that cruel Fourth of July night. I didn't just die—my whole being melted away into ashes in slow motion. There were countless hours, which turned into days, when I was just in bed, lifeless, my back awfully sore from being slumped longer than necessary, my hair tangled, my stomach in violent protest.

I came back to life slowly, in jilted stages. It was a process, recreating the connection to the world, to my family, to Kyle, to myself, as I broke the surface and floated back up. Only to be crushed again by my divorce. In hindsight, the prospect of divorce killed me for a second but brought me back to a fuller existence. Then Liam came into my life. But there were too many ghosts of the past. Too many scraps. We had already lost, even before we could begin. The odds were against us. It was better to kill it now. And so, I was dead again inside.

Kyle and I decided to stay home for Christmas Eve. It was easier to handle each other than our inquisitive mothers. Even with his music blasting in the background, all I could hear was a ricocheting silence. I had already mentally reduced any expectations of a joyous night. Christmas stopped being that to us. We had Chinese takeout. The chow mein and kung pao chicken paired perfectly with his beer, while the honey walnut shrimp went well with my pinot grigio.

"Have you made up your mind about Gulfport?" Kyle's tone was so earnest that I deliberated on every word I was about to put out there.

"Gulfport is just one of the things we have to worry about. Or make a decision on. Honestly, it's us, Kyle. Do you really believe that we still have a chance?"

"It's not a simple yes or no, Kate. But we won't know if we don't try harder."

My thoughts were interrupted as Kyle's phone started ringing. I saw how he scowled at the phone before he rejected the call. I would usually ignore this, but his pale face suddenly turned red, so it bothered me for a second. I was about ready to continue disregarding it until his phone beeped to indicate a text message.

"You should get that if it's important," I said blankly.

"No," Kyle said almost immediately then added, "It can wait. Back to us, Kate. What is it you want?"

I looked around the house. I even closed my eyes to summon myself to want something. There was nothing here that I wanted. No one that I needed.

"I want us to be happy, both of us. Whether together or separately."

I paused as I tried to muster enough strength. I prepared myself as I released something that I'd bottled up inside me. "We have not been happy for a long time now. I think we both deserve it. We are good people. Why can't we be happy?" I finally crumbled.

Between my sobbing and his phone ringing, Kyle seemed stumped. He finally answered his phone, and with an angry voice said, "I'll have to call you back!"

"How long has that been going on?" I asked slowly but with even breaths.

"What?"

I watched Kyle intently as I began to realize that this was our chance to come clean. To free ourselves from the guilt, from punishing ourselves further. "Let's get a divorce, Kyle."

"Why?" His voice was in the median between angry and agitated. "Because of the phone call?"

"No. It was bound to happen. I think we're just waiting for June to naturally separate us."

Kyle didn't say a word. He took a swig of his beer and proceeded to finish his bowl of chow mein.

This had been rehearsed in my head numerous times. I had come to realize that the only thing that had stopped me was the fear of hurting Kyle. It became apparent that I had to come clean to free myself, and to encourage him to do the same.

"I've been with someone, Kyle. It just happened."

Kyle inhaled so deeply it would seem he was taking in all the air for himself, leaving me with nothing. He took another swig of his drink, then stood up and walked to the fridge to get another bottle of cold beer. He went to one of the kitchen drawers to get the bottle opener and pivoted the lever to remove the cap. He tossed the thing back to the drawer and slammed it violently to close it. He then went back to his seat. Crossed his arms. After a few more minutes, he finally spoke.

"Is it over?"

I nodded, avoiding any discriminating stare.

"Do you love him?" The crack in his voice betrayed him.

I gently nodded again.

"What do you mean it just happened?"

"When I went to Manila."

"Christ! It's my fault." He dropped both elbows on the table and slumped over, with his forehead braced by both palms as he shook his head. I could see that he was wrestling with all sorts of emotions. "I slept with Snow once. I was confused—I was angry at you. It happened right after our last fight, just before I asked for a divorce. I shouldn't have said that. I didn't mean it. It was a desperate act. I pushed you away. I pushed you too much. I thought . . . I thought it would be good for us to move. Maybe we can be happier in Mississippi."

"Was that Snow calling?" I calmly asked while I stared down on the ground, both of us avoiding eye contact.

"Yes. But it's not what you think. We've just been talking. She's probably getting ahead of herself again. I'm not gonna leave you for her, Kate."

"Kyle, I'm in love with someone else." I leaned in closer as I said this. I never imagined saying these words to the father of my son.

With both hands, he covered his face and let out a loud grunt. "So what do we do now, Kate?" I had seen Kyle angry in the past. I was used to it. When our son died, he was angry for a long time. It didn't startle me. For the most part, I wished I could help him get through it. But how could I, when I was living in an apocalypse myself.

"I think we've known for a while. We just haven't been honest with each other, with ourselves."

"So, you just met the guy in the Philippines. I mean, how? Who's the guy?"

"It's Liam."

As soon as I said his name, Kyle thumped the table with his fist, and all the beer bottles rattled. He stood and walked out of the room.

• • •

I was emptying an extra-large brown corrugated box half my height. The depth was not ideal. It was in fact a mistake. I had unpacked more than a third of its contents. That word, emptying. It was more than a task. It was an end goal.

Kyle and I went through with our divorce. We settled the whole thing in the middle of spring. We sold our house before he left for Gulfport. I heard that Snow went with him. My mom had been so worried about me. I was fine, I kept on telling her. But the way she looked at me, it was as though I was worse than a springtime flower that withered before it could bloom. It was not like it was the end of the world. It was more of not knowing where and how to proceed. Imaginably, she could see through that.

When Kyle hugged me for the last time as he said goodbye, I was happy to unburden him of his guilt. "You deserve someone who will take care of you. I didn't know about Snow when I went with Liam, so you should stop blaming yourself for that. We tried with all we've got, Kyle. We just have to move forward now, separately." My words were wiser than what I could possibly know.

"I hope you'll find yourself, Kate. I'll always think of you. I think the world of you. And I wish for your happiness." He whispered this to my ear and squeezed me tight once more before his arms let go of me. I watched him walk away. For good. I mourned for us that night. I grieved over the people that we were once—Willy's mother and father.

• • •

All my moving boxes were now empty, ready to be recycled. I took the last item out of the deep box. The final piece of my life that I had yet to unload. I could tell from the shape that it was a framed art piece. I carelessly unwrapped the protective kraft paper, which accidentally ripped in the center, revealing the photograph. Liam's gift. The pristine white oval water tub sitting outdoors among young bamboo trees. That held naked lovers as they cleansed the filth off their bodies. Picturesque bamboo trees that can withstand heat and moisture, and its spirited timbers that can be cut without killing whatever will remain of it.

I got a washcloth to wipe the frame of any fingerprints and smears. Have you ever stared at a photo long enough that it deluged you with the past? A lost fragment that you regrettably wished to go back to. And that during moments of recollection, you began to understand, perhaps in a hundred silent ways, that it was once real. Because you still carried the pain. The pain was the evidence that it was real.

Life had presented me with a throng of twists and turns. I had also been through heaven and hell. The regrets I had were all on me. A bottleneck of misgivings fettered inside like a blood clot preceding a heart attack. Should I continue leaving my fate to chance again?

As I moved around the small room to figure out where to place the photograph, I examined the back side to see what kind of hook it came with. There was none. The sticker read "Easel Stand Inside."

Perhaps it was best not to start forming holes on the wall anyway. I stood next to my nightstand, contemplating a location for the photograph. I thought I should test to see how I would feel once I positioned it there. Using a butter knife to unscrew the corners, I gently detached the backside of the frame, and in doing so an envelope with my name dropped on the floor.

My hands were shaking as I read Liam's letter.

To my dearest Kate,

I can't get through life thinking that I caused you pain. If I could only take back those words I said, or go back to that day, I would make everything right. I may have lost you for good, and this fear is breaking me. Knowing I had a chance, and suspecting that might have been my one and only.

I can think of a number of instances we could have met. The fact that none of them shaped up was a relief. Not knowing then what we know now allowed us to have our moments.

I'm in love with you, Kate. More than what my words can explain. More than the silence I could bear.

I believe we were meant to meet. Don't you feel this way too? It was easy for us, right away. It felt right. The only thing that ever stopped me from pursuing this was the burden you'll have to carry, or that it may break you miserably. They say to love means to seek the good for the other person. The last thing I want is to cause you more heartache.

But I can't help but ask if there will be a time in the future when you will allow me to see you again?

Please don't close the door completely on us. I'll be somewhere, anywhere, anytime, always waiting. Save me from my loneliness. Let me love you. Let me make you happy. God, I have missed you.

Love,
Liam

CHAPTER 21

When the Red Light Turned Yellow

"Two roads diverged in a yellow wood,
and sorry I could not travel both."

—Robert Frost

T he school year was about to end, which had always been the busiest time for Liam. But he was not about to complain. The students had always taken priority in his life, even when the school took away time from his personal life. Not that he was having much luck in that department. He was on standby, a course of action he decided he was willing to take on, however long it took. For now, all he could ever do was check his phone and email. And he did, regularly. As soon as he woke up. During lunch. Right before bed. Or right before calling it a day as he checked his watch and started getting ready to leave his office.

It was not the email he was waiting for—not from that sender, at least.

• • •

June 2, 2017

It could have easily been me on that day. I could have been there instead of Pete inside that cargo plane that blew up. It could have been me if you didn't switch schedules that day.

I always had this sense of obligation to repay you for saving my life somehow. I didn't realize it would turn into a burden more than a vow. Well, everything stops right here. We are even. We are done.

—Kyle

Liam leaned back in his chair. He inhaled his worries deeply and shut his eyes. He deliberated over every word in the email, speculating as to how things transpired that made Kate reveal this to Kyle. Most importantly, he was contemplating the effect it had on Kate. How was she? Was she safe? Why had she not sent a message? Despite her words being as clear as day when they said their goodbyes, Liam had continued to harbor a glint of hope inside him. Because that was all he had left, and it was hard to let go of that faint flicker of faith.

All Liam could do at that moment was bank on how he remembered Kyle, hoping his moral fiber would not allow him to hurt his wife. Hoping it had not changed—the Kyle he knew would never hit a woman. Not that it reassured Liam completely. But enough to convince himself not to send a frantic message to Kate just yet.

CHAPTER 22

When Food for Thought Was Served for Lunch

"The liberty we knew, avoided like a dream.
Too wide for any night but Heaven, if that indeed redeem."

—Emily Dickinson

"Kate, let's have lunch."

It was barely six in the morning. The phone call startled me to such a degree that I was unable to answer back. Of course, it was not a question. And there was no reason to turn it down.

We were meeting at a bistro—Oliver's. Nothing fancy. Closer to squalid, in my honest opinion. Even at noon, yellow lights were already moderately dimmed. Pints of beer were ordered like flavored water. As soon as I walked in, the musky waft suggestive of a long day's toil greeted my face. These hardworking men who were lined up at the bar certainly looked like they were done for the day.

I had never been to Oliver's. And I could see why. It spoke of wild and mischief. But everyone seemed to be patrons here because when a non-regular walked in, heads turned.

"I'm meeting someone. She might be already here." In my most inconspicuous voice.

"Are you meeting Doris?" the hostess asked welcomingly.

"Yes." I had never been happier to hear Doris's name. As I marched, covered behind the waitress, I couldn't help but wonder why she loved hanging out in this place. She ate here every day. She was here more than she was at her own bakeshop.

A brawny man with a beard so thick he could very well play Santa stood up to say there was an empty spot next to him.

"Hey, she's with Doris." The waitress looked back and gave me a reassuring smile. "Ignore him, hon."

The man sheepishly fluttered his hand as if to say, "Forget it."

I'm gonna kill Doris. I tried adjusting my breathing.

Tucked in the corner booth was my friend, seated stoically. Doris looked up and forced a smile. Because she was seemingly not in the best of moods, I decided not to give her grief for dragging me to her watering hole.

"What's up, Doris? You haven't shown up to the bakeshop for weeks now. My boss might fire you." I said this teasingly, with a smirk, but the sarcasm was lost on her.

"You should get the soup here. The only thing I come here for. And the pint."

Doris had always been a great friend. We grew closer during the years after I lost Willy. She had been a widow for so long and without children. I had been her family these past few years.

I was seventeen when I started working for Doris. She was someone I always regarded with admiration. With her great sense of humor and fun energy, Doris was always the life of the party. Her voice was authoritative when required, and charismatic when appropriate. Her laugh was infectious. In my eyes, Doris had always been that forty-year-old boss who took me under her wing like the daughter she never had.

When I noticed that her hand was shaking as she scooped the soup, I began to view Doris as if I was suddenly given a different pair of eyes. In a flash, I noticed how her body seemed really feeble, as if she had aged twice as fast in these past few weeks compared to how she gracefully skipped adding years over the past decade.

"Is everything okay, Doris?"

Doris gazed at me lovingly. Her eyes stayed on mine. With a forced smile that didn't really conceal her quivering lips, swallowing what seemed like a big lump in her throat, my friend took a long, deep breath. When she closed her eyes for a brief second, a teardrop escaped out of her green eyes. The pair that used to evince so much *oomph* was now acquiescent.

"I've been going through dialysis. I'm sorry I didn't tell you sooner."

My reaction, evidenced in the way I covered my mouth with both hands, as if stopping a monster from escaping, was the reason Doris kept this from me. It brought dark clouds of memories—the saddest and harshest kind.

Have you ever run down the stairs so fast that you accidentally skipped two or three steps, landing on one foot peculiarly hard, so that your stomach lurched from the sudden scare? When you were snapped out of the initial fright, you were amazed and grateful to be still standing, bones intact, your face not flat on the ground, and you let out a sigh of relief. The fact that Doris was able to meet me for lunch was a good indication, I convinced myself.

"It's working, right?" I flashed a smile at my friend. Pushing her to share the good news of a recovery. "You're going to be fine now, that's why you're telling me this. Right?"

"I'm dying, Kate." Her voice was faint but her words echoed in my ears violently.

Whenever I watched actors in films cry a waterfall without batting an eyelash, I always thought it was what acting workshops had trained them to do. I didn't realize it could happen to me. I felt my cheeks get wet within seconds, my collarbone now a pool of tears. But I felt so helpless, like someone had taken all my energy and power, so much so that not even my eyelids could move.

Doris extended her hands and laid them palms up and open. It was an invitation to reach out, so I clasped her hands within mine.

"Don't be too sad, Kate. I'm ready." I slumped my weeping face on our fastened hands as I wailed very loudly to the surprise of all the regulars at Oliver's.

• • •

Doris died in hospice care, on a day one week apart from Willy's death anniversary. I made sure that she was not alone. I was holding her hand. When she said she was ready, she meant that all her dying wishes had been legally documented so it would proceed as planned. Like the DNR, and how she wanted the celebration of life at Oliver's, and including how she had transferred everything she owned to her employees.

The memorial at Oliver's happened one week after her body was cremated. My second trip to Doris's favorite watering hole was less dramatic. It was my turn to watch my mom acting the way I had. This time, I was better prepared for the ambience and the regulars, most of whom were friends of Doris, and all of them gathered here to pay their respect to one great lady.

"Shower. Comb hair and those beards. And for the love of Oliver's, use an after-shave. Please celebrate my life. Don't be sad. At the end of the day, promise, promise, promise me to live life to the fullest. If you were invited, it's because, believe it or not, you were my friend." Doris had even written her own memorial invite.

The room was alive with stories about Doris. The space, as expected, reeked of booze and after-shave cologne. Everyone was friends, or ended up being one at the party. Jim, fake-Santa-Jim, became one of my buddies. He no longer petrified me. Marge, the hostess, was as sweet as the day we met. She called everyone "hon" but she was the real honey.

"Kate?"

I turned around when I heard my name. The man with slicked-back hair, wearing a nice black jacket paired with denim pants, handed me a business card. "Take this. Doris talked to me about offering my services to you should you need help with the bakery. I own a small construction company. Doris requested, actually threatened, to turn up from her grave if I charge you an enormous bill, so I will do the most I can, whatever you need. I intend to keep my promise to Doris. She was a lovely woman."

"Thank you" was the only thing I found the strength to say. I held on to the business card just as I held on to his promise. In truth, I was drained from all of this, starting from day one, at that lunch when Doris revealed her sickness to me. Caring for a terminally ill friend was a different kind of agony. In a way, I was partly praying that it would end for her soon, because keeping her alive in that kind of pain was not a miracle at all. It was a poor quality of life, full of cruelty. Nobody deserved that—I could only see that now about my own son's situation. I had just been too desperate to keep him alive.

"Hey, how are you holding up?" Frank, our talented baker—the longest and perhaps the most loyal employee who never took a day off in his life—asked me. I had never seen him outside the bakeshop, without his hat and apron, so it was strange, the good kind of strange, to see a different side of him. When I shrugged my shoulders to mean however the receiver would take it, Frank continued. "You know, Doris gave me her house."

I smiled, almost tempted to say that was the only silver lining I found in this whole ordeal because, frankly, Frank was hardworking and deserved every bit of generosity his luck would afford him.

"She gave me a letter that explained why the house was a better deal for me than the bakeshop. She asked that I stay for as long as I could with the shop. Doris didn't need to ask me that, Kate. I will be as loyal to you as I was with Doris. You're like a daughter. Anyway, I just wanted to check that you're holding up okay."

"Enjoy the house, Frank. I am sincerely happy that it ended up with you. It's a beautiful home."

Frank was a family man with some grown children. His wife had always been a stay-at-home wife while raising their six children. Then the grandkids. Work had begun at one in the morning every single day for the past twenty years. The house was fully paid off, so I understood why Doris had left that instead of the bakeshop to Frank. He was a great baker, but it would make more sense that he would finally own a property, rather than leave him one with a financial burden.

The bakeshop was, in many ways, an intense load to receive. The property still had some years of payments left. I was worried over whether I could truly afford paying the remainder of the mortgage solely from the store's income. And that the bakeshop had four employees, including me, didn't ease the burden and responsibility. I had to make sure the shop stayed afloat. Which sadly meant that, in all good faith, I couldn't sell the shop. Which meant I couldn't leave Oxnard. Which meant I couldn't be with Liam.

CHAPTER 23

When Seasons Changed

"Then give to the world the best you have,
and the best will come to you."
—Madeline Bridges

I t was Labor Day, almost two months since I took over the bakeshop. Even as a working student, my work ethic had always been a reason to celebrate this holiday. Now that I was a business owner, with most of my brain consumed with the economics of things, it was easily justifiable to start my holiday morning with a shot of whiskey as I proclaimed to Frank, "Yes, today is about us diligent workers!" I was hailing myself for coming out victorious, if not still sane, after all these trying months. And so, I did. Had that shot of whiskey to Frank's amusement. And proclaimed my sentiments in my loudest grunt.

"Yaw . . . yikes." I was trying to jiggle away the bitterness from the shot glass. "Should we do another round, Frank?" I was honestly hoping that he would refuse my fake challenge. When he shook his head, I made another proclamation. "Whiskey, I conclude, is not for me!" I was already in giggles and apparently a little tipsy after that one shot. Frank and I were both in the back laughing when the bell rang.

"You okay getting that customer, or are you really drunk off of that tiny shot?"

"Pfft . . ." I rolled my eyes at Frank—at the ridiculousness of his insinuation—even though I did feel his remark might not be that far from the truth.

I strode to the front, smacking my lips wet to remove the still lingering taste of alcohol in my mouth, then fought to hide the silly smirk in my attempt not to look like a happy drunk as I yelled, "I'll be right with you." As I switched my apron out for a cleaner one, with both hands struggling with making ends meet, literally, as I tied up the straps, I walked forward, looking down at my steps as if watching the ground was helping me focus on the task of fastening the apron.

"You need help with that?"

My heart skipped a beat. Nippy cold air brushed all the hair on my skin. My head felt fuzzy for one split second. One blink before I looked up to find the face to the familiar voice. One half step before I ran directly into the arms, which have, unknowingly to the owner of those arms, held me together these past months.

Liam was probably expecting a warm hello, even a signed hello. But perhaps not me running the way I did toward him, and certainly not the no-kidding-you-are-here embrace. When I let go, Liam's breathtaking eyes were glassy, and his perfect nose made a few short sniffs. But his wide smile, *oh the smile*, was one that could easily wash off all the bitterness in the world, including the aftertaste of whiskey in my mouth.

"I hope this means you're happy I'm here. Because I'm beyond heaven to finally see you again."

I raised both hands flat facing my chest and moved them in forward-circular, upward-downward motion as I said "happy."

"Are you sure you didn't mean to sign milking the cow?"

My bewildered eyes, which have probably never opened up so big, sent Liam laughing.

When did I ever sign that? I gently jabbed his bicep. Not a sign, but it had been my way of saying "I surrender" to him. Liam stepped closer to give me his version of "I missed you." His hug was never tight, always leaving a little wiggle room, as if he was mindful of never wanting to suffocate me. Still, I felt the pounding of his chest uniting with mine.

"Everything alright here?" Frank had come out of the kitchen to check on me.

"Oh yes, of course." I turned around and said to Frank, "I want you to meet . . . Liam."

I finger-spelled F-R-A-N-K to Liam.

"Hi, Frank. Pleasure to meet you," he said, offering a handshake.

Frank offered a quick nod while receiving Liam's hand. He then said to me, "I might have seen this guy a few times in his car watching the shop—I didn't think much of it, but I must say I was a little tempted to report him to the cops. Now I'm glad I didn't." Frank could only offer a smile after his revelation.

When I curbed a gasp by covering my mouth with one hand, Liam asked, "What is it?"

"Later." I said this while signing.

With Liam sitting in one of the corner tables, my motions were a little overwrought. I parted my hair to the side, then fixed it back to the earlier way within seconds. Or I was wiping the same spot over and over until my distracted motions were interrupted by a phone alert. "Are you scraping off the color of the table?" was Liam's message.

And when I found myself losing my train of thought as I chatted with a customer, I finally decided, "The shop is done for the day." Frank had left, business was slow, and I could think of better ways to spend my afternoon. I turned the lock on the front door, flipped the "Open" sign to "Closed," and left the store, four hours earlier than usual, with Liam.

He left his rental car parked outside the shop and rode with me back to my apartment. It was during times like this when Liam said things I was never expected to reply back to.

"Happy Anniversary. It's been a year."

My lips pressed into a line, although loosely crooked, and resembling a smirk. But what was not evident to Liam were the tingles in my skin and the defeated heart that seemed to have come around at this moment.

It had been a year for us—Liam and me—even without being sanctioned as something that was allowed, or possible. A week that left us weakened for the remainder of the year. A secret that revealed to us more than what the world had wanted to let us in on. A passion that left us perplexed, wanting nothing but each other. Yes, it was that kind of year, with every single day spent waiting, wishing, then waiting again.

It was just mid-day but my apartment was super dark, except for some strips of light creeping through those small gaps between the louvers from that one window in my tiny studio apartment. My mom had begged me to move back home, but I had declined profusely. I needed my own space. The apartment had felt perfect. It was clean, fairly new, and what I could afford.

When I switched on the light, I felt Liam standing behind me with his arms slowly moving around my waist. Earlier, his only question for me was about the status of my relationship with Kyle. When I told him I was divorced, Liam hadn't asked a single thing, up until now.

"Can I stay with you tonight?"

I turned around and immediately received his kiss—the sexiest, sweetest, smoothest kind there was. The sort that wiped away all the aches and cynicism in one tick. The stroke that healed me back to existence.

We made love on my miniscule daybed. Though it was the perfect size for me and the apartment, I couldn't say the same for my tall visitor. All the same, neither one of us wanted to let go of the other's grip.

"What did Frank say that shocked you earlier?"

This had almost slipped my mind. It was a little upsetting to learn that Liam had been in town a few times but had never told me. I rose from the bed, taking the short blanket with me—a little revenge for his secret visits. It was perhaps a wicked thing to do, and I zealously looked back to see how exposed I had left him, but never mind—he was faster, the pillow already covering my favorite parts.

Returning with a pen and paper, I wrote, "Frank said he almost called the cops on you the few times he saw you at the parking lot. Care to explain?"

Liam cleared his throat and sat up on the bed. "I came once in July, a couple of weeks after I received Kyle's email saying we were no longer friends. I wanted to see for myself that you were okay, that he didn't hurt you or anything. You were hardly at the shop, so I ended up asking one of the storekeepers about you. It seemed she kept her promise not to tell you."

I interrupted by explaining that it was probably at a time when I was busy taking care of Doris. Liam nodded.

"Then, for this trip, I'd been here in town for over a week, but I wanted to see how things were with you. I didn't want to show up and interrupt your life . . . not if you had moved on."

"Thank you for showing up."

My heart was warm and melting for this man. I kissed him, as a show of gratitude. And the kiss was about to lead to something more when the doorbell rang. I ran to the peephole and jumped out of my skin as I saw my mother behind the door. I frantically picked up all the clothes on the floor on my way back to Liam and wrote, "My mom is here."

"I want to meet her," Liam said before putting on his pants, so I wrote, "Soon as you have pants on."

Liam laughed then grabbed me closer so he could whisper, "It will be okay. Relax. I'll beg if I have to get your mom to like me."

After taking two very long and slow inhale-exhale stretches, I opened the door with a wide smile, all my teeth showing up for my mom.

"Hello, Mom."

"Why did you close your store? Are you si—sick?"

When my mother dramatically suspended the last word, I knew even without looking behind me that Liam had decided to join us at the door.

"Mom, please come in and meet my friend."

Liam eagerly offered his hand, even when he must have known social graces dictated to wait for the lady to offer her hand first in a handshake. This tall Caucasian guy who had seen some tough times—like the war—suddenly was practically cowering next to this petite Asian mother. It was almost like a David and Goliath moment—and this was just the start of crazy.

My apartment, despite its size, allowed for a small round table in the middle of the room. Thankfully I had three chairs, so I didn't have to take my mom anywhere near my bed. I grabbed my pen and paper and joined the two of them, who were both seated with hands folded on their chests and looking anywhere but at each other.

My mom was peering curiously at the notepad, so I quickly explained. "Liam is profoundly Deaf from an accident when he was in the military."

My mom slowly took in the information, then finally asked, "Is he your boyfriend?"

With both knuckles together, palms facing inward, and thumbs sticking up while gesturing them in an upward downward motion as if the thumbs were birds cooing each other, I turned to Liam with a questioning look on my face. Like my mother, I was also curious to find out where Liam's surprise visit was leading us to.

"I want to marry Kate."

That was the last thing I had expected to come from his mouth.

My mother and I, in chorus, started choking—it was as if his declaration had gone down the wrong pipe. This sent Liam scrambling to figure out what was where in my kitchen as he fetched two glasses of water. This little bomb had taken our breath away.

When my mother regained her composure, I was still massaging my chest to calm the blood pumping in waves that were still crashing inside me. My mom proceeded to write a note to Liam, then promptly rose and left. Because she was smart enough to know not to direct the invitation at me, she got the response she wanted—Liam readily nodded as soon as he read it.

"Please join us for dinner tonight."

When I finally read the note, with wide eyes, I couldn't help but yell. "You said yes to dinner?"

Liam laughed. He didn't need to hear what I said—he knew exactly what I meant from what I imagined was the incredulous expression that registered on my face.

"Why did you not let me take care of getting out of dinner?" I was less agitated as Liam started stroking my neck in an effort to relax me.

"Because I want to have that dinner actually and meet your family."

"You don't know what you've signed up for," I warned him in writing.

"Are we not going to talk about the fact that I just asked for your hand in marriage?"

I turned around to plant a soft kiss on his lips. Then I laid my head on his shoulder for support. I was basking in the splendor of being reunited with him. Because this was all I needed. The evidence that what we had was real. That Liam was here with me now was enough underwriting—I didn't need any other obligatory acts or documents to feel secure in what it was we had.

Moments later, when Liam was still waiting for my answer, he decided to clarify the status of his proposal. "What? You don't want to get married? You don't want to marry me?"

"I can't leave Oxnard. You can't leave your school. How do we do this marriage thing?"

Perhaps Liam should not have pursued this conversation because writing this down made this sentiment into a more lucid reality. The coughing bout should have been enough of a red flag.

We left the marriage talk open-ended as we got ready to head out to dinner. It was like a bottle of good wine that's nearly done. Instead of chugging it straight to the bottom, it was more judicious to put the cork back to save it for another great celebration, rather than to waste it all in one go. We both knew it was best to save the wedding talk for another time.

Barry and Mom's house smelled like Thanksgiving as soon as we walked in. Cool citrus and lemongrass mixed with a warm roasted garlic scent, which competed with the sweetness of vanilla and burnt caramel. There was also that refreshing, earthy scent of jasmine and *pandan* steaming off from my mom's tried and tested rice cooker.

Barry opened the door to greet us and offered Liam a handshake. There was no need to sign his name, as Liam had done his research ahead of time.

As soon as I saw the feast on the table, I corrected myself in assuming this was reminiscent of the beloved American holiday dinner. This was clearly *barrio fiesta*.

"A traditional Filipino dinner." I was saying this to myself as I pondered why she decided to cook this spread.

Barry must have seen me gazing intently at the table. He casually moved to my side and whispered, "Beats me. Either your mom wants to test his endurance for Filipino food or she's testing if you're pregnant."

I chuckled while looking at the nicely plated babyback ribs sprinkled with green onions and arranged neatly on a bed of roasted garlic, lemon slices, quail eggs, and a small puddle of adobo juice.

When my mom entered the dining room carrying a big ceramic bowl, Liam moved like a soldier to get it off her hands. He gently laid the dish in one corner. Inside the bowl was an assortment of colors, from the purple eggplants to the lime-green—in my opinion, slimy-green—okras, and white rounded radishes, all swimming along with the fish head, belly, and tail. And with blanched kale and Swiss chard on the side.

"Mom, thank you for cooking adobo. I miss the smell of the garlic and vinegar." My mom looked back at me as I said this, so I gave her a wink.

"I'm glad." She smiled wide, knowing she got caught.

When my mom arrived at the table again, holding a generous square of leche flan oozing in caramel sauce, my stepdad motioned his hand to say have a seat.

Liam promptly offered his compliment to my mom. "Thank you for cooking us dinner. I love Filipino cuisine."

Barry quelled a grin while my mom nodded in defeat.

But sweet Adora had more than one trick up her sleeve. When she turned on the smart TV mounted in front of their dining table and mirrored her phone with it, I instantly knew this was going to be a long dinner.

"Siri, where did you eat Filipino cuisine?"

I was delighted to see the amount of effort my mom put in as an attempt to communicate with Liam, and was amused at how appalled she was when Siri answered her question with, "I don't understand."

Liam offered to fix this by going to an app that would allow my mom to dictate, with the text projecting on the screen, while leaving Siri out of the conversation.

"So, I tried the local cuisine when I was in Manila, just as I do on every trip."

"When were you in Manila?" My mom was even more probing.

I could already feel the train that was about to hit me, but I was not scared.

"Last year. That was when Kate and I met."

I could feel my mother's eyes waiting to meet mine while I kept myself busy inspecting the fish for any bones. It required focus, which I kept at diligently, even when my mother tried getting my attention by clearing her throat and saying my name under her breath.

She only left me alone once she saw that I was signing as a way to communicate with Liam, pointing my right index finger from my right eye down to my left hand as I slid it through an open palm. "Inspect." I said the word for my parents to understand as well.

"For what? Fishbones?" When I nodded, Liam said, "Don't worry about that."

In the years that my mom and stepdad had been together, I learned to accept Barry. I had seen how well he took care of my mother and adored her beyond sufficiency.

After my mother, it was Barry's turn to open up his bag of tricks. When my stepdad started signing, I was beyond thrilled. I was happy to have someone in my family who would be able to include Liam in dinner conversations, regardless of how minimal the extent of communication. I watched them until it became clear to me how impressive Barry's knowledge of ASL was—the two were just flowing with conversation. At that point, I turned to my mom, ready to finally tell her what she knew all along. *You did good, Mom.*

CHAPTER 24

When You're Ready to Taste the Sweetness of the Watermelon

"Time has not changed the joys we knew;
the summer rains or winter snows."

—Edgar A. Guest

I volunteered to push the metal cart. This unexpected late morning trip with Mom felt more like an ambush. A trap which I had been trying to decipher since her phone call that same morning—an invitation for a quick errand to the supermarket, with her. Grocery shopping was something she did by herself, for as long as I could remember. She knew which aisle to go to, and what brands to get. She never allowed someone else to buy her groceries, or took anyone with her, as it would only slow her down.

At the end of her call, she promised that it would be "sweet and swift"—her exact words.

The fact that I was wearing my yoga pants but missing my yoga class, and was being forced to learn the tricks to pick the sweetest watermelon, was one of the many ambiguities of the day. Just like how I was supposed to distinguish deep sound from the regular kind as I patted on the watermelon's underbelly. How does a deep sound *sound?* From the belly of the watermelon! I always used the carmine red color as an indication of sweetness. Of course, this was always an insight after the fact, or after the purchase.

"If you can't tell by tapping, then choose the heaviest."

"Mom, they all weigh the same," I said coolly, although I was more like an overheated oven inside, in frustration.

"No, you should be able to tell. If they feel lighter, it means they're not as juicy."

I had grasped over the years the providence of choosing my battles with my mom. Who cares if this watermelon turns out to be a disappointment? It was still considered early in the day to argue with Mom. I kept on nodding so we could move away from the fruit section. Even when my hands were at the handlebar of the cart, my mom seemed to be maneuvering this as she was dragging the cart in the direction she wanted to go.

"Kate, do you know what's the best brand for eggs?"

"Mom," I had to let out a weak protest. "What are we doing here? Seriously."

"Kate, you have to know all these things before you move away. It will be hard teaching you this when we're in different states."

"What? Where am I going?" I was perplexed with what she just said, the evidence written on me as my mom snapped back, "I hope the fruits we bought are not as sour as your face now."

She pulled the cart from its standstill as we arrived at the canned vegetables and pasta aisle. My mom continued our discussion as if we were in the privacy of her living room.

"I don't think it's wise to let people wait for you for long. No matter how much they love you or are patient with you. Even Liam."

"What are you saying, Mom?"

"This watermelon here—once we get home, let's slice it open and taste. If it's sweet, I think it's a sign that you're ready to pick your own watermelon. Your future watermelons with Liam."

At this point, I also no longer cared if other people could hear us. "Will you be okay if I leave California?" I had never considered moving away, so I was taken aback to hear that my mom had contemplated this.

"Kate, I'm stronger than you give me credit for." She replied instantly, as if she had prepared herself for this conversation.

"Mom, we always try to spare you from any disappointments— Dad did . . . Barry, me—this is probably why you feel you're strong on your own, at least stronger than what is true."

My mom did not look back at me to reveal how she took this in. She kept mum for the next two aisles, so I let her digest it. We kept walking through the more crowded aisles.

"I know about Diday. Did it break me? No." She shared this like she was simply giving me a secret recipe. When my tongue retreated to safety, afraid to catch fire, my mom continued. "That's why you should never keep anything from me. I am much stronger than you think I am."

"How did you know?"

"I heard rumors years ago, I ignored it. But when you left your father's house, he panicked. He had to explain everything to me."

"I'm sorry I didn't have the courage to tell you."

"I know. That's why this time, I urge you—have the courage to follow what's right. To follow your heart. To follow Liam."

When it became my turn to be tight-lipped, my mom carted me along the baking section.

After I saw Mom grab a Jiffy biscuit mix, my thoughts abandoned the deliberation in my head. "All . . . these . . . years," I said with much exaggeration, then paused so that my mom would turn around to prod me to keep talking. When she did, I went on. "I thought those biscuits were made from scratch."

My mom indulged me with a faint grin. "Kate . . ." Mom gripped the end of the cart to stop. "Sometimes—in fact, often—easy is just as good. Things don't need to be complicated."

Right in between the shelves loaded with feminine hygiene products and baby diapers, I understood why I had always sought my mom's wisdom and approval—she was my candle vendor. She had discerned everything in my life even before it made sense to me. But I was in no mood to lay out the red carpet to her favorite line—*I told you so.*

On our drive back, after we hauled eight brown bags of groceries into her car, I decided to go all in and open the can of worms. It seemed like the kind of day for it. "Have you forgiven Dad?"

"For getting involved with Diday? Yes." I had to hand it to my mom—she was never startled at the questions I lobbed at her. "For breaking your heart? I don't know, Kate. You have to tell me—help me on that one."

And here I was thinking that I was dealing with an amateur, only to realize that the can of worms had crept up on me more than it had my mom. "You know what I've been meaning to ask you?"

"Yeah?"

"Why you never took me grocery shopping till now."

My mother laughed so hard I was worried we'd collide into something. She was the kind of driver who never allowed her eyes to alight anywhere else other than the road. To watch her head wobble with an uncontrollable giggle was not an encouraging scene.

"Mom!" I was not happy to be the killjoy, but I had to kill her joy at the moment. "Watch the road, Mom!"

"Oh, you relax. I'm an awesome driver."

"No, not awesome. Flawsome."

She quit giggling. "What does that mean?" Because she was driving, my mom could not look at me, but I knew how much she wanted to give me a scowl. I heard it in her tone.

"You are awesome but not without flaws."

"I'll take it. It doesn't sound bad at all. And not far from the truth."

I wanted to hug my mom but we were not the demonstrative hug-out-of-the-blue kind. Plus, I didn't want to distract her, so all I could manage to do was let out a heavy sigh.

• • •

As I helped my mom put away the things we got from the store, I suddenly felt silly thinking I was going to rely on a fruit to decide for me. At any rate, I made light of it as I saw Mom load up the watermelon onto a chopping board.

"What if that turns out to be sour?"

Mom placed both of her hands on the large oval fruit to keep it from rolling. "Kate, I have yet to find a sour watermelon. Maybe watered-down or bland, but never sour. Besides, I was teaching you a technique, to make a smart guess at best, not fortune telling."

"I know, Mom," I interrupted. "I was just joking."

"Here's what's not funny . . ."

I caught myself about to roll eyes as a habit, like what I was used to do whenever a lecture was about to hit me, so I made a great effort to look straight at my mom as I waited for her to speak.

"Don't let anything or anyone decide for you. It has to be what you want. And never stop pursuing a dream, or an opportunity, because you're trying to be considerate of others. I certainly don't want to see you miserable and missing Liam on my account."

• • •

Two days later and after much pondering, I was convinced that a short text message should be a good start to rebuilding my relationship with my father.

After a few back-and-forth taps on delete, return, and space, I sent my dad a text. "For whatever it's worth, I wanted to tell you that my trip to Manila was the best thing that happened to me in recent years, especially the chance to see you again."

It didn't take long to receive his reply. "It's twenty years late, but I'm sorry for walking away. I always think of you every day. You're the one thing I'm proud of, even when I'm not much as a father."

In the end, if I had hoped for my mom to forgive my dad, then it had to start from me. Which meant I had to start forgiving my father.

CHAPTER 25

When the Holiday Colors Are Back

"Bring me the sunset in a cup. Reckon the
morning's flagons up . . . Write me how many
notes there be. In the new robin's ecstasy."

—Emily Dickinson

The holiday colors are the same ones—the evergreen that represents life, the bright red for unconditional love, the silver white bringing light to the darkness, the golden yellow for gifts, and the amaranth purple for the king. They have been the same every year. Only, I was too misted up to see the sparkles.

But I see them now. I can smell the sweetness and warmth of eggnog once more—that wild amalgamation of whiskey, vanilla, cinnamon, and nutmeg. I can hear the roars and bellows of sleigh bells and tambourine harmonizing with cheerful lyrics about love, joy, and peace. I can feel the cold air that sets a nice equilibrium to the balminess within. And I can finally touch my own skin and feel it. I am no longer numb.

It is my turn to visit Liam and spend the Christmas holiday meeting his family and friends in Louisville. I have always spent all my winters in Southern California, so I have never experienced a snowy winter. I have never walked through piles of snow so deep I worry my feet might sink in—but at the same time feel confident that I can pull them out and keep going. I am suddenly reminded of Diday and how she cautioned me from consuming all the tidbits of the *halo-halo*, because I would be left with nothing but crushed ice. It is, after all, what my life has been. I have to scoop everything out if I am to have a clean slate. All the crushed ice inside me has to melt so that my spirit can flow through. So that love can flow through.

Liam prepares the fireplace in his living room, where I am bundled with a vibrant quilted cotton throw that I can only assume came from one of his South Asia trips. I am in one of two bronze leather wingback armchairs, where I am closer to the charcoal-steel panels mounted around this industrial-looking fireplace. Everything else is vanilla and oak in the room, from the big, oatmeal-colored tufted French sofa that can hold at least four bodies, to the creamy vintage rug that speaks of a culture that is intricate in its handwoven strokes and is laid perfectly over the dark-stained oak flooring. The flanking glass wall that separates this room from a lovely, lush outdoor space allows for brightness to come in. Liam, if this room represents his way of life, is always soaking in natural light. That's why he can be as easy as a light blue sky, or warm and intense like the midday sun, or a quiet shadow waiting for dusk.

Liam leaves the room and returns with two cups of hot drink. His is coffee while mine is vanilla chai tea. He invites me to the larger seat so that we are now facing the outdoor grounds and a full moon in its ripest expression, which I have not seen for a while now.

"Are you really freezing?"

Literally I am freezing, but also thawing inside, if that makes any sense at all. All the same, I bob my head wildly because a special moment like this deserves nothing short of grand gestures, just like the one I am about to showcase.

I sign "I have a surprise for you, don't laugh" to Liam, then proceed to play "Sexual Eruption" from my phone. I am erotically dancing the first few lines—if erotic means sloppily swaying my hips or doing a strip-tease rendition of my festive "Ho, Ho, Ho" red socks—until the chorus when I finger-spell the title words. Only then does this crazy, crazy act make sense to Liam. From that point on, he just can't stop laughing.

When we are both finally able to settle down, and once my breathing stabilizes from this heart-pumping, dance-signing rendition, I go up to Liam, look him in the eye, then motion my right-hand fist in an upward-downward motion like a head nodding "yes."

Liam cups my face with both hands and kisses me. Once our lips part, I proceed to give Liam a notecard that reads:

"Nothing is more important than starting a life together, with you. Frank offered to buy me out, and I'm finally comfortable moving away from my mom. I realize I was hovering around her, perhaps my way of protecting her. I can move here, build a new me. Build another bakeshop. Call my mom from here. I can do all this anywhere, as long as I am with you. I'm saying yes to you, Liam. I want to marry you."

Liam folds the note and places it back in the envelope. He puts it on the accent table and begins to explain his plan for us. "I've been working on setting up another school in Ventura because I know that's home for you. They're mostly in the planning stage, and it may take years to shape up. But I promise you, Kate, I'll give up everything I have, including the school, if one day you feel homesick and need to be closer to your mom. Thank you for making it possible for us to be together."

Liam gets up and takes a hardbound book. He opens the book halfway, removing a photograph. It is of Willy, when he was a newborn. I remember writing the notes on the back of the photograph—quoting a line from the kite book he sent my son. I remember telling Kyle to send the photograph to his friend, not even bothering to ask for his friend's name. I reminisce on how much Willy loved that book. I remember the strokes of my hand when writing the caption, and how I was so careful not to splotch the ink, blowing air on it before putting it in an envelope, with the "to" and "from" left blank, for Kyle to take care of.

"It was a photograph I've carried with me, even without meeting your son. I took comfort in knowing there was this little boy growing up with a father. An aspect I had trouble reconciling with Pete's family, because he was the one who died in that accident. Because I couldn't do much on that end, I focused on your son. The gift he was given—to have a father. Hearing, uninjured, walking again. That part helped me heal. Thank you for sending me this photograph."

It's not that I have stopped thinking about my son. Grief is something hard to talk about. I don't know how to share his story with anyone without the intense surge of pain, of getting engulfed with my grief. And this is the moment when I finally feel at peace. Perhaps because time has healed me somehow, or Liam's love protects me from the pain. Or knowing that my son played an important role in someone's healing without even knowing about it. In the end, I have to listen from within to even have a chance at healing. At being heard. And listening.

My thoughts are suddenly interrupted when I see movements behind the glass wall. They are just children, so I am not too startled. They carry placards and, as they form a straight line facing us, I read the message—"Will me? marry you." Liam motions his hand so the two kids holding the "me?" and "you" cardboards can switch.

Once the message reads correctly, Liam turns to me with a small box in his hand. He opens it, reveals the ring, and slides it onto my finger.

"I'm not going to ask anymore, because . . . well, first of all, I already asked you a few times. You never gave me an answer, so I thought I'd let my nephews and nieces ask with their puppy faces. Then earlier, even before I'm able to propose again, you said yes. I don't know if our timing is still off, but let me seize the moment now and put the ring on you!"

I know now more than ever, that actions speak louder than words, so what better way to say yes than to give Liam one mammoth kiss.

Liam's mother and the rest of the family walked into the living room to join us. It is heartwarming to be welcomed by his family right away. Heartwarming like the sweet scent of pine trees even in the spring, and the earthiness come autumn. Their embrace feels as if I have always been a part of them. I am in the midst of learning everyone's name when a thought hits me and my hand instinctively covers my wide-open mouth. I turn to Liam, who seems to have read my mind, as he gives a weak shrug. Then his mom pulls me in closer to her but away from the rest as she says softly, "Don't worry. I had everyone hide in the laundry room. And I asked the kids to cover their ears too."

Throughout the evening, I watch his entire family sign while talking. Even the little boys and girls. Even in a crude kind of way, as basic as my signing. But we manage to understand each other. Manage to laugh at jokes. Even Liam gets the jokes. Or perhaps he laughs because he is really happy. Just as I am.

Liam pulls me away from the gathering. "Come on, let's step outside for a bit. It doesn't seem like my family plans on leaving anytime soon." I accept his invitation despite a small protest in me against what I know will be freezing temperatures on the other side of the door. I put my jacket and gloves on and wrap a scarf around my neck. Liam grabs a shopping bag and takes out a fluffy pair of earmuffs. He comes closer to me and puts them on me.

"In case it's very cold for you, or if I talk really loud, this might help too."

With my left arm sideways facing me, I sway my right palm across, above my left forearm but closer to my chest. I motion my right hand as if I'm flipping a music page over or waving it like an orchestra conductor. I always forget to tell him how his voice is music to my ears. I could go on and on about his sexy voice that melts me away, but his family is still around so I will save it for a private conversation or a text.

We walk to a corner gazebo and sit on a gray wicker sofa. It is nice and quiet—not the sad or eerie sort. It's the calming kind of quiet.

"Can I tell you what sign name we could use for you so we don't have to finger-spell Kate? Only if you like."

I smile in anticipation.

Liam shows me the letter K on his right fingers as he uses it to touch his right shoulder, then moves it across his chest to the left shoulder while explaining. "Instead of an index finger, we should use the letter K to sign 'we' because Kate is now a we—she is your Kate and my Kate."

I come up to Liam for a quick kiss but he pulls me in to sit on his lap. "So Kate," he says, "when are we going back to Tokyo?"

Acknowledgments

I admire my two teenage kids for their wit—often funny, definitely snappy and spontaneous, but sometimes, snappy like grouchy. From time to time, I wonder if I didn't have to translate things in my head, if I could be as zesty as they sound. Since English is not my native language, I always think in Filipino, then articulate my thoughts in English. This is the reason why I love writing more than speaking. The challenges, even barriers, in communication are familiar and personal experiences. This is the inspiration for some of the characters in *A Hundred Silent Ways*.

I want to express my gratitude to my college best friends, Maan Gabriel and Lace Goodwin. They are more than mentors, critics, and cheerleaders. They are some of the essence of this book. If I have to put both in a phrase, it would be this—The sun and the moon give out equal brilliance.

To my editor Ava Coibion, who pushed for better story structure and reminded me to slow down whenever my writing was like a marathon—either too fast-paced or too long and drawn out. You were a gift to the manuscript.

To the rest of the amazing team behind this project—Tyler LeBleu, who kept us all accountable in production; my lead editor, Jessica Reyes, who by coincidence also became a sounding board for Kate's voice; Elizabeth Brown for her trenchant copy edit; Tonya Trybula; and David Endris.

To Neil Gonzalez and his creative team, who captured the core of the story through the vibrant artwork of the book cover. And to Chelsea, Tiffany, and the rest of the Marketing and Distribution teams at Greenleaf Book Group for their guidance and expertise.

To my early readers, Jill Angel and Pamela Hom, who gave great insights and honesty. I am also grateful for Katherine Cornish and Zachary Lotane for helping me understand Liam better.

To Mr. Brian Galetto, who allowed me to use his work "Speak Up" from his thought-provoking poetry book *Not So Simple*, which was the recipient of the 2019 California Book to Action Award.

To the wonderful Gizle Manchester, a friend and fellow Fil-Am. Thank you for letting me borrow your impressive photographs, which I used in some of my marketing efforts. Luckily for me, I wrote some passages that I hope complemented your art.

To my supportive family—kuya Mick and younger brother Marc; Tita Arlene, Tita Ian, Tita Yolly, and other real-life titas; my sisters-in-law Lei, Ate Kit, and Mel; my cousins Me-Ann, Aaron, Carl, and Angelo; TJ, Maki, and JC; my families in San Diego and Manila, and good friends in Oxnard, as well as Luisa; Lenie, and other Fil-Am friends—all of whom I surprised one day with the announcement that I wrote a novel.

Although my grandfather, Super Lolo Pilo, never got to witness this milestone in my life, I'm still grateful for the many years he was given to be with us. When I was five or six years old, he had the proudest clap in the room even when I sang out of tune. My kids had this kind of moment with him as well.

To my parents, Arseng and Mila, who truly believe in me, more than I deserve. They gave me the courage to dream, and never said my dreams were foolish or impossible.

To Patrick, who never complained whenever we had to do takeouts because I wanted to work on my book. Your love and understanding mean the world to me.

And to you holding a copy of this book—even if it seemed too sad in the beginning, I hope I gave you a heartwarming story. Knowing that someone enjoyed reading *A Hundred Silent Ways* is my happy ending.

About the Author

Mari Jojie was born and raised in Manila, Philippines. It was home for half of her life. Married to a retired US Navy senior chief, she is grateful to have experienced living in other parts of the world, including these two very contrasting cities—the historic and authentic Napoli, and the forward-thinking and innovative Dubai. Currently, she resides in Oxnard, California, with her husband, daughter, and son.

Tokyo was the first foreign city she ever visited. She was there for one week as an exchange student. Her fondest memory from that trip was a cup of creamy soup her host family served upon her arrival. For a teenage girl from a tropical country experiencing her first cold winter night, that warm, hearty soup tasted like heaven.

Many, many years later, in an attempt to finish the leftover baked ham from Thanksgiving, she put together some canned Campbell's soup, heavy cream, corn, onion, and cubed ham in a crockpot. Three hours after, she had a flashback of that night as soon as she tasted her extempore dish. She unknowingly created the soup she thought was an impossible thing to ever taste again. She's a believer of providential full circle.

A Hundred Silent Ways is her debut novel. And was for several years, just an imagined courage beyond her wishful thinking.